The Critics Praise
HOUSEKEEPING
By Marilynne Robinson

"This novel is a winner: in fact, I can't remember reading a first novel that has impressed me so much. Like most works of art, it can be savored in layers. . . . Ms. Robinson uses language so fresh, so direct, so accurate and essential that practically every sentence is worth close attention. Her humor is of the kind that makes you smile from its truth, and she selects and sifts her perceptions like a poet. This is a novel to prize and reread."

—Elizabeth Jane Howard,
Harper's and Queen, London

"*Housekeeping* is a quiet, humorous, beautiful book filled with what I can only call the ecstasy of wisdom. . . . I think that there are few first novels published since mid-century to compare with *Housekeeping* for sheer perfections of language and for conveying what it means to be human. It is a work of pure grace."

—John Hawkes

"The richness and variety and the peculiarity of tone Marilynne Robinson sustains are masterful; I found the characters absorbing and disturbing."

—Mary Gordon

"A STORY AS RIVETING AND TAUT AS THE PLUNGE OF A TRAIN FROM BRIDGE TRACKS INTO LAKE WATER BELOW, THE BOOK'S PRIMAL AND HAUNTING INCIDENT . . ."

HOUSEKEEPING
A Novel by
Marilynne Robinson

"A stunningly moving story about a devastated family. . . . The narrator (Ruth) is a dreamy, gangly girl who has lost so much so young—her mother (suicide), father (disappeared) and grandmother. Robinson's most dazzling creation, though, is the girl's Aunt Sylvie, a 35-year-old misfit who flirts with suicide, then finds her salvation in a tenuous family life with the teenager. Robinson infuses the tale with offbeat humor, but the enduring impact of this book lies in its pervasive understanding of tragedy."

—*People*

HOUSEKEEPING

A haunting, lyrical novel of great beauty, steeped in images of earth, water, air and fire. *Housekeeping* is the story of Ruth . . . and her memories as she grows from childhood to adulthood on a brooding glacial lake in the towering mountains of Idaho; out of ashes and dissolution—a new self and life emerge . . .

"*HOUSEKEEPING* IS AN ACHIEVEMENT OF MAGNITUDE, A DEFT DEFIANCE OF CONVENTION, A SINGULAR BOOK."

—*Commonweal*

HOUSEKEEPING

Marilynne Robinson

BANTAM BOOKS
NEW YORK • TORONTO • LONDON • SYDNEY • AUCKLAND

For my husband,
and for James and Joseph, Jody and Joel,
four wonderful boys

HOUSEKEEPING
A Bantam Book / published by arrangement with
Farrar, Straus & Giroux Inc.

PRINTING HISTORY
Farrar, Straus & Giroux edition published January 1981
Serialized in Harper's Magazine February 1981
Bantam edition / March 1982
11 printings through August 1988
Bantam trade edition / May 1989

All rights reserved.
Copyright © 1980 by Marilynne Robinson.
Cover art copyright © 1987 by Fred Marcellino.
No part of this book may be reproduced or transmitted in any form or by any means,
electronic or mechanical, including photocopying, recording, or by any information
storage and retrieval system, without permission in writing from the publisher.
For information address: Farrar, Straus & Giroux Inc.,
19 Union Square West, New York, N.Y. 10003.

Library of Congress Cataloging-in-Publication Data

Robinson, Marilynne.
Housekeeping.

I. Title.
PS3568.03125H6 1989   813'.54   88-47880
ISBN 0-553-34663-6 (pbk.)

Published simultaneously in the United States and Canada

Bantam Books are published by Bantam Books, a division of Bantam Doubleday Dell
Publishing Group, Inc. Its trademark, consisting of the words "Bantam Books" and
the portrayal of a rooster, is Registered in U.S. Patent and Trademark Office and in
other countries. Marca Registrada. Bantam Books, 666 Fifth Avenue, New York,
New York 10103.

PRINTED IN THE UNITED STATES OF AMERICA
FG   0 9 8 7 6 5 4 3 2 1

HOUSEKEEPING

1

My name is Ruth. I grew up with my younger sister, Lucille, under the care of my grandmother, Mrs. Sylvia Foster, and when she died, of her sisters-in-law, Misses Lily and Nona Foster, and when they fled, of her daughter, Mrs. Sylvia Fisher. Through all these generations of elders we lived in one house, my grandmother's house, built for her by her husband, Edmund Foster, an employee of the railroad, who escaped this world years before I entered it. It was he who put us down in this unlikely place. He had grown up in the Middle West, in a house dug out of the ground, with windows just at earth level and just at eye level, so that from without, the house was a mere mound, no more a human stronghold than a grave, and from within, the perfect horizontality of the world in that place foreshortened the view so severely that the horizon seemed to circumscribe the sod house and nothing more. So my

grandfather began to read what he could find of travel
literature, journals of expeditions to the mountains of
Africa, to the Alps, the Andes, the Himalayas, the Rockies.
He bought a box of colors and copied a magazine lithograph
of a Japanese painting of Fujiyama. He painted many more
mountains, none of them identifiable, if any of them were
real. They were all suave cones or mounds, single or in
heaps or clusters, green, brown, or white, depending on the
season, but always snowcapped, these caps being pink,
white, or gold, depending on the time of day. In one large
painting he had put a bell-shaped mountain in the very
foreground and covered it with meticulously painted trees,
each of which stood out at right angles to the ground, where
it grew exactly as the nap stands out on folded plush. Every
tree bore bright fruit, and showy birds nested in the boughs,
and every fruit and bird was plumb with the warp in the
earth. Oversized beasts, spotted and striped, could be seen
running unimpeded up the right side and unhastened down
the left. Whether the genius of this painting was ignorance
or fancy I never could decide.

One spring my grandfather quit his subterraneous house,
walked to the railroad, and took a train west. He told the
ticket agent that he wanted to go to the mountains, and the
man arranged to have him put off here, which may not have
been a malign joke, or a joke at all, since there are
mountains, uncountable mountains, and where there are
not mountains there are hills. The terrain on which the
town itself is built is relatively level, having once belonged
to the lake. It seems there was a time when the dimensions
of things modified themselves, leaving a number of puz-
zling margins, as between the mountains as they must have
been and the mountains as they are now, or between the
lake as it once was and the lake as it is now. Sometimes in
the spring the old lake will return. One will open a cellar
door to wading boots floating tallowy soles up and planks

and buckets bumping at the threshold, the stairway gone from sight after the second step. The earth will brim, the soil will become mud and then silty water, and the grass will stand in chill water to its tips. Our house was at the edge of town on a little hill, so we rarely had more than a black pool in our cellar, with a few skeletal insects skidding around on it. A narrow pond would form in the orchard, water clear as air covering grass and black leaves and fallen branches, all around it black leaves and drenched grass and fallen branches, and on it, slight as an image in an eye, sky, clouds, trees, our hovering faces and our cold hands.

My grandfather had a job with the railroad by the time he reached his stop. It seems he was befriended by a conductor of more than ordinary influence. The job was not an especially good one. He was a watchman, or perhaps a signalman. At any rate, he went to work at nightfall and walked around until dawn, carrying a lamp. But he was a dutiful and industrious worker, and bound to rise. In no more than a decade he was supervising the loading and unloading of livestock and freight, and in another six years he was assistant to the stationmaster. He held this post for two years, when, as he was returning from some business in Spokane, his mortal and professional careers ended in a spectacular derailment.

Though it was reported in newspapers as far away as Denver and St. Paul, it was not, strictly speaking, spectacular, because no one saw it happen. The disaster took place midway through a moonless night. The train, which was black and sleek and elegant, and was called the Fireball, had pulled more than halfway across the bridge when the engine nosed over toward the lake and then the rest of the train slid after it into the water like a weasel sliding off a rock. A porter and a waiter who were standing at the railing at the rear of the caboose discussing personal matters (they were distantly related) survived, but they were not really witnesses in any sense, for the equally sound reasons that the darkness was impenetrable to any eye and that they had been standing at the end of the train looking back.

People came down to the water's edge, carrying lamps. Most of them stood on the shore, where in time they built a fire. But some of the taller boys and younger men walked out on the railroad bridge with ropes and lanterns. Two or three covered themselves with black grease and tied themselves up in rope harnesses, and the others lowered them down into the water at the place where the porter and the waiter thought the train must have disappeared. After two minutes timed on a stopwatch, the ropes were pulled in again and the divers walked stiff-legged up the pilings, were freed from their ropes and wrapped in blankets. The water was perilously cold.

Till it was dawn the divers swung down from the bridge and walked, or were dragged, up again. A suitcase, a seat cushion, and a lettuce were all they retrieved. Some of the divers remembered pushing past debris as they swam down into the water, but the debris must have sunk again, or drifted away in the dark. By the time they stopped hoping to find passengers, there was nothing else to be saved, no relics but three, and one of them perishable. They began to speculate that this was not after all the place where the train left the bridge. There were questions about how the train would move through the water. Would it sink like a stone despite its speed, or slide like an eel despite its weight? If it did leave the tracks here, perhaps it came to rest a hundred feet ahead. Or again it might have rolled or slid when it struck bottom, since the bridge pilings were set in the crest of a chain of flooded hills, which on one side formed the wall of a broad valley (there was another chain of hills twenty miles north, some of them islands) and on the other side fell away in cliffs. Apparently these hills were the bank of still another lake, and were made of some brittle stone which had been mined by the water and fallen sheerly away. If the train had gone over on the south side (the testimony of the porter and the waiter was that it had, but by this time they were credited very little) and had slid or rolled once or twice, it might have fallen again, farther and much longer.

After a while some of the younger boys came out on the bridge and began to jump off, at first cautiously and then almost exuberantly, with whoops of fear. When the sun rose, clouds soaked up the light like a stain. It became colder. The sun rose higher, and the sky grew bright as tin. The surface of the lake was very still. As the boys' feet struck the water, there was a slight sound of rupture. Fragments of transparent ice wobbled on the waves they made and, when the water was calm again, knitted themselves up like bits of a reflection. One of the boys swam out forty feet from the bridge and then down to the old lake, feeling his way down the wall, down the blind, breathless stone, headfirst, and then pushing out from the foot. But the thought of where he was suddenly terrified him, and he leaped toward the air, brushing something with his leg as he did. He reached down and put his hand on a perfectly smooth surface, parallel to the bottom, but, he thought, seven or eight feet above it. A window. The train had landed on its side. He could not reach it a second time. The water bore him up. He said only that smooth surface, of all the things he touched, was not overgrown or hovered about by a cloud of something loose, like silt. This boy was an ingenious liar, a lonely boy with a boundless desire to ingratiate himself. His story was neither believed nor disbelieved.

By the time he had swum back to the bridge and was pulled up and had told the men there where he had been, the water was becoming dull and opaque, like cooling wax.

Shivers flew when a swimmer surfaced, and the membrane of ice that formed where the ice was torn looked new, glassy, and black. All the swimmers came in. By evening the lake there had sealed itself over.

This catastrophe left three new widows in Fingerbone: my grandmother, and the wives of two elderly brothers who owned a dry-goods store. These two old women had lived in Fingerbone thirty years or more, but they left, one to live with a married daughter in North Dakota and the other to find any friends or kin in Sewickley, Pennsylvania, which she had left as a bride. They said they could no longer live by the lake. They said the wind smelled of it, and they could taste it in the drinking water, and they could not abide the smell, the taste, or the sight of it. They did not wait for the memorial service and rearing of the commemorative stone, when scores of mourners and sightseers, led by three officers of the railroad, walked out on the bridge between handrails mounted for the occasion, and dropped wreaths on the ice.

It is true that one is always aware of the lake in Fingerbone, or the deeps of the lake, the lightless, airless waters below. When the ground is plowed in the spring, cut and laid open, what exhales from the furrows but that same, sharp, watery smell. The wind is watery, and all the pumps and creeks and ditches smell of water unalloyed by any other element. At the foundation is the old lake, which is smothered and nameless and altogether black. Then there is Fingerbone, the lake of charts and photographs, which is permeated by sunlight and sustains green life and innumerable fish, and in which one can look down in the shadow of a dock and see stony, earthy bottom, more or less as one sees dry ground. And above that, the lake that rises in the spring and turns the grass dark and coarse as reeds. And above that the water suspended in sunlight, sharp as the breath of an animal, which brims inside this circle of mountains.

It seems that my grandmother did not consider leaving. She had lived her whole life in Fingerbone. And though she never spoke of it, and no doubt seldom thought of it, she was a religious woman. That is to say that she conceived of life as a road down which one traveled, an easy enough road through a broad country, and that one's destination was there from the very beginning, a measured distance away, standing in the ordinary light like some plain house where one went in and was greeted by respectable people and was shown to a room where everything one had ever lost or put aside was gathered together, waiting. She accepted the idea that at some time she and my grandfather would meet and take up their lives again, without the worry of money, in a milder climate. She hoped that he would somehow have acquired a little more stability and common sense. With him this had so far not been an effect of age, and she distrusted the idea of transfiguration. The bitter thing about his death, since she had a house and a pension and the children were almost grown, was that it seemed to her a kind of defection, not altogether unanticipated. How many times had she waked in the morning to find him gone? And sometimes for whole days he would walk around singing to himself in a thin voice, and speak to her and his children as a very civil man would speak to strangers. And now he had vanished finally. When they were reunited, she hoped he would be changed, substantially changed, but she did not set her heart on it. Musing thus, she set out upon her widowhood, and became altogether as good a widow as she had been a wife.

After their father's death, the girls hovered around her, watched everything she did, followed her through the house, got in her way. Molly was sixteen that winter; Helen, my mother, was fifteen; and Sylvie was thirteen. When their mother sat down with her mending, they would settle themselves around her on the floor, trying to be comfortable, with their heads propped against her knees or her chair, restless as young children. They would pull fringe off the rug, pleat her hem, pummel one another sometimes, while they talked indolently about school or worked out the endless minor complaints and accusations that arose among them. After a while they would turn on the radio and start brushing Sylvie's hair, which was light brown and heavy and hung down to her waist. The older girls were expert at building it into pompadours with ringlets at ear and nape. Sylvie crossed her legs at the ankles and read magazines. When she got sleepy she would go off to her room and take a nap, and come down to supper with her gorgeous hair rumpled and awry. Nothing could induce vanity in her.

When suppertime came, they would follow their mother into the kitchen, set the table, lift the lids off the pans. And then they would sit around the table and eat together, Molly and Helen fastidious, Sylvie with milk on her lip. Even then, in the bright kitchen with white curtains screening out the dark, their mother felt them leaning toward her, looking at her face and her hands.

Never since they were small children had they clustered about her so, and never since then had she been so aware of the smell of their hair, their softness, breathiness, abruptness. It filled her with a strange elation, the same pleasure she had felt when any one of them, as a sucking child, had fastened her eyes on her face and reached for her other breast, her hair, her lips, hungry to touch, eager to be filled for a while and sleep.

She had always known a thousand ways to circle them all around with what must have seemed like grace. She knew a thousand songs. Her bread was tender and her jelly was tart, and on rainy days she made cookies and applesauce. In the summer she kept roses in a vase on the piano, huge, pungent roses, and when the blooms ripened and the petals fell, she put them in a tall Chinese jar, with cloves and thyme and sticks of cinnamon. Her children slept on starched sheets under layers of quilts, and in the morning her curtains filled with light the way sails fill with wind. Of course they pressed her and touched her as if she had just returned after an absence. Not because they were afraid she would vanish as their father had done, but because his sudden vanishing had made them aware of her.

When she had been married a little while, she concluded that love was half a longing of a kind that possession did nothing to mitigate. Once, while they were still childless, Edmund had found a pocket watch on the shore. The case and the crystal were undamaged, but the works were nearly consumed by rust. He opened the watch and emptied it, and where the face had been he fitted a circle of paper on which he had painted two seahorses. He gave it to her as a pendant, with a chain through it, but she hardly ever wore it because the chain was too short to allow her to look at the seahorses comfortably. She worried that it would be damaged on her belt or in her pocket. For perhaps a week she carried the watch wherever she went, even across the room, and it was not because Edmund had made it for her, or because the painting was less vivid and awkward than his paintings usually were, but because the seahorses themselves were so arch, so antic and heraldic, and armored in the husks of insects. It was the seahorses themselves that she wanted to see as soon as she took her eyes away, and that she wanted to see even when she was looking at them. The wanting never subsided until something—a quarrel, a visit—took her attention away. In the same way her daughters would touch her and watch her and follow her, for a while.

Sometimes they cried out at night, small thin cries that never woke them. The sound would stop as she started up the stairs, however softly, and when she reached their rooms she would find them all quietly asleep, the source of the cry hiding in silence, like a cricket. Just her coming was enough to still the creature.

The years between her husband's death and her eldest daughter's leaving home were, in fact, years of almost perfect serenity. My grandfather had sometimes spoken of disappointment. With him gone they were cut free from the troublesome possibility of success, recognition, advancement. They had no reason to look forward, nothing to regret. Their lives spun off the tilting world like thread off a spindle, breakfast time, suppertime, lilac time, apple time. If heaven was to be this world purged of disaster and nuisance, if immortality was to be this life held in poise and arrest, and if this world purged and this life unconsuming could be thought of as world and life restored to their proper natures, it is no wonder that five serene, eventless years lulled my grandmother into forgetting what she should never have forgotten. Six months before Molly left she was already completely changed. She had become overtly religious. She practiced hymns on the piano, and mailed fat letters to missionary societies, in which she included accounts of her recent conversion and copies of two lengthy poems, one on the Resurrection and another on the march of Christ's legions through the world. I have seen these poems. The second speaks very warmly of pagans, and especially of missionaries, ". . . the angels come to roll away / The stone that seals their tomb."

Within six months Molly had arranged to go to China, to work for a missionary society. And even while Molly belabored the air with "Beulah Land" and "Lord, We Are Able," my mother, Helen, sat in the orchard talking softly and seriously to a certain Reginald Stone, our putative father. (I have no memory of this man at all. I have seen photographs of him, both taken on the day of his second wedding. He was apparently a pale fellow with sleek black hair. He appears at ease in his dark suit. Clearly he does not consider himself the subject of either photograph. In one he is looking at my mother, who is speaking to Sylvie, whose back is to the camera. In the other he appears to be grooming the dents in the crown of his hat, while my grandmother, Helen, and Sylvie stand beside him in a row, looking at the camera.) Six months after Molly left for San Francisco and thence for the Orient, Helen had set up housekeeping in Seattle with this Stone, whom she had apparently married in Nevada. My grandmother, Sylvie said, was much offended by the elopement and the out-of-state marriage, and wrote to tell Helen that she would never consider her genuinely married until she came home and was married again before her mother's eyes. Helen and her husband arrived by train with a trunk full of wedding clothes, and with a box of cut flowers and champagne packed in dry ice. I have no reason to imagine that my mother and father were ever prosperous, and so I must assume that they went to some trouble to salve my grandmother's feelings. And yet, according to Sylvie, they did not spend twenty-four hours in Fingerbone. Relations must have mended somewhat, however, because a few weeks later Sylvie, in a new coat and hat and shoes, with her mother's best gloves and handbag and valise, left for Seattle by train to visit her married sister. Sylvie had a snapshot of herself waving from the door of the coach, sleek and young and proper. As far as I know, Sylvie only came home once, to stand where Helen had stood in my grandmother's garden and marry someone named Fisher. Apparently no snapshots were made of this event.

One year my grandmother had three quiet daughters and the next year the house was empty. Her girls were quiet, she must have thought, because the customs and habits of their lives had almost relieved them of the need for speech. Sylvie took her coffee with two lumps of sugar, Helen liked her toast dark, and Molly took hers without butter. These things were known. Molly changed the beds, Sylvie peeled the vegetables, Helen washed the dishes. These things were settled. Now and then Molly searched Sylvie's room for unreturned library books. Occasionally Helen made a batch of cookies. It was Sylvie who brought in bouquets of flowers. This perfect quiet had settled into their house after the death of their father. That event had troubled the very medium of their lives. Time and air and sunlight bore wave and wave of shock, until all the shock was spent, and time and space and light grew still again and nothing seemed to tremble, and nothing seemed to lean. The disaster had fallen out of sight, like the train itself, and if the calm that followed it was not greater than the calm that came before it, it had seemed so. And the dear ordinary had healed as seamlessly as an image on water.

One day my grandmother must have carried out a basket of sheets to hang in the spring sunlight, wearing her widow's black, performing the rituals of the ordinary as an act of faith. Say there were two or three inches of hard old snow on the ground, with earth here and there oozing through the broken places, and that there was warmth in the sunlight, when the wind did not blow it all away, and say she stooped breathlessly in her corset to lift up a sodden sheet by its hems, and say that when she had pinned three corners to the lines it began to billow and leap in her hands, to flutter and tremble, and to glare with the light, and that the throes of the thing were as gleeful and strong as if a spirit were dancing in its cerements. That wind! she would say, because it pushed the skirts of her coat against her legs and made strands of her hair fly. It came down the lake, and it smelled sweetly of snow, and rankly of melting snow, and it called to mind the small, scarce, stemmy flowers that she and Edmund would walk half a day to pick, though in another day they would all be wilted. Sometimes Edmund would carry buckets and a trowel, and lift them earth and all, and bring them home to plant, and they would die. They were rare things, and grew out of ants' nests and bear dung and the flesh of perished animals. She and Edmund would climb until they were wet with sweat. Horseflies followed them, and the wind chilled them. Where the snow receded, they might see the ruins of a porcupine, teeth here, tail there. The wind would be sour with stale snow and death and pine pitch and wildflowers.

In a month those flowers would bloom. In a month all dormant life and arrested decay would begin again. In a month she would not mourn, because in that season it had never seemed to her that they were married, she and the silent Methodist Edmund who wore a necktie and suspenders even to hunt wildflowers, and who remembered just where they grew from year to year, and who dipped his handkerchief in a puddle to wrap the stems, and who put out his elbow to help her over the steep and stony places, with a wordless and impersonal courtesy she did not resent because she had never really wished to feel married to anyone. She sometimes imagined a rather dark man with crude stripes painted on his face and sunken belly, and a hide fastened around his loins, and bones dangling from his ears, and clay and claws and fangs and bones and feathers and sinews and hide ornamenting his arms and waist and throat and ankles, his whole body a boast that he was more alarming than all the death whose trophies he wore. Edmund was like that, a little. The rising of the spring stirred a serious, mystical excitement in him, and made him forgetful of her. He would pick up eggshells, a bird's wing, a jawbone, the ashy fragment of a wasp's nest. He would peer at each of them with the most absolute attention, and then put them in his pockets, where he kept his jackknife and his loose change. He would peer at them as if he could read them, and pocket them as if he could own them. This is death in my hand, this is ruin in my breast pocket, where I keep my reading glasses. At such times he was as forgetful of her as he was of his suspenders and his Methodism, but all the same it was then that she loved him best, as a soul all unaccompanied, like her own.

So the wind that billowed her sheets announced to her the resurrection of the ordinary. Soon the skunk cabbage would come up, and the cidery smell would rise in the orchard, and the girls would wash and starch and iron their cotton dresses. And every evening would bring its familiar strangeness, and crickets would sing the whole night long, under her windows and in every part of the black wilderness that stretched away from Fingerbone on every side. And she would feel that sharp loneliness she had felt every long evening since she was a child. It was the kind of loneliness that made clocks seem slow and loud and made voices sound like voices across water. Old women she had known, first her grandmother and then her mother, rocked on their porches in the evenings and sang sad songs, and did not wish to be spoken to.

And now, to comfort herself, my grandmother would not reflect on the unkindness of her children, or of children in general. She had noticed many times, always, that her girls' faces were soft and serious and inward and still when she looked at them, just as they had been when they were small children, just as they were now when they were sleeping. If a friend was in the room her daughters would watch his face or her face intently and tease or soothe or banter, and any one of them could gauge and respond to the finest changes of expression or tone, even Sylvie, if she chose to. But it did not occur to them to suit their words and manners to her looks, and she did not want them to. In fact, she was often prompted or restrained by the thought of saving this unconsciousness of theirs. She was then a magisterial woman, not only because of her height and her large, sharp face, not only because of her upbringing, but also because it suited her purpose, to be what she seemed to be so that her children would never be startled or surprised, and to take on all the postures and vestments of matron, to differentiate her life from theirs, so that her children would never feel intruded upon. Her love for them was utter and equal, her government of them generous and absolute. She was constant as daylight, and she would be unremarked as daylight, just to watch the calm inwardness of their faces. What was it like. One evening one summer she went out to the garden. The earth in the rows was light and soft as cinders, pale clay yellow, and the trees and plants were ripe, ordinary green and full of comfortable rustlings. And above the pale earth and bright trees the sky was the dark blue of ashes. As she knelt in the rows she heard the hollyhocks thump against the shed wall. She felt the hair lifted from her neck by a swift, watery wind, and she saw the trees fill with wind and heard their trunks creak like masts. She burrowed her hand under a potato plant and felt gingerly for the new potatoes in their dry net of roots, smooth as eggs. She put them in her apron and walked back to the house thinking, What have I seen, what have I seen. The earth and the sky and the garden, not as they always are. And she saw her daughters' faces not as they always were, or as other people's were, and she was quiet and aloof and watchful, not to startle the strangeness away. She had never taught them to be kind to her.

A total of seven and a half years passed between Helen's leaving Fingerbone and her returning, and when she did finally return it was on a Sunday morning, when she knew her mother would not be at home, and she stayed only long enough to settle Lucille and me on the bench in the screened porch, with a box of graham crackers to prevent conflict and restlessness.

Perhaps from a sense of delicacy my grandmother never asked us anything about our life with our mother. Perhaps she was not curious. Perhaps she was so affronted by Helen's secretive behavior that even now she refused to take notice of it. Perhaps she did not wish to learn by indirection what Helen did not wish to tell her.

If she had asked me, I could have told her that we lived in two rooms at the top of a tall gray building, so that all the windows—there were five altogether, and a door with five rows of small panes—overlooked a narrow white porch, the highest flight of a great scaffolding of white steps and porches, fixed and intricate as the frozen eke of water from the side of a cliff, grainy gray-white like dried salt. From this porch we looked down on broad tarpaper roofs, eave to eave, spread like somber tents over hoards of goods crated up, and over tomatoes and turnips and chickens, and over crabs and salmons, and over a dance floor with a jukebox where someone began playing "Sparrow in the Treetop" and "Good Night, Irene" before breakfast. But of all this, from our vantage, we saw only the tented top. Gulls sat in rows on our porch railing and peered for scavenge.

Since all the windows were in a line, our rooms were as light as the day was, near the door, and became darker as one went farther in. In the back wall of the main room was a door which opened into a carpeted hallway, and which was never opened. It was blocked, in fact, by a big green couch so weighty and shapeless that it looked as if it had been hoisted out of forty feet of water. Two putty-colored armchairs were drawn up in a conversational circle. Halves of two ceramic mallards were in full flight up the wall. As for the rest of the room, it contained a round card table covered with a plaid oilcloth, a refrigerator, a pale-blue china cupboard, a small table with a hotplate on it, and a sink with an oilcloth skirt. Helen put lengths of clothesline through our belts and fastened them to the doorknob, an arrangement that nerved us to look over the side of the porch, even when the wind was strong.

Bernice, who lived below us, was our only visitor. She had lavender lips and orange hair, and arched eyebrows each drawn in a single brown line, a contest between practice and palsy which sometimes ended at her ear. She was an old woman, but she managed to look like a young woman with a ravaging disease. She stood any number of hours in our doorway, her long back arched and her arms folded on her spherical belly, telling scandalous stories in a voice hushed in deference to the fact that Lucille and I should not be hearing them. Through all these tales her eyes were wide with amazement recalled, and now and then she would laugh and prod my mother's arm with her lavender claws. Helen leaned in the doorway, smiled at the floor, and twined her hair.

Bernice loved us. She had no other family, except her husband, Charley, who sat on her porch with his hands on his knees and his belly in his lap, his flesh mottled like sausage, thick veins pulsing in his temples and in the backs of his hands. He conserved syllables as if to conserve breath. Whenever we went down the stairs he would lean slowly after us and say "Hey!" Bernice liked to bring us custard, which had a thick yellow skin and sat in a copious liquid the consistency of eyewater. Helen was selling cosmetics in a drugstore, and Bernice looked after us while she was at work, though Bernice herself worked all night as a cashier in a truck stop. She looked after us by trying to sleep lightly enough to be awakened by the first sounds of fist fights, of the destruction of furniture, of the throes of household poisoning. This scheme worked, though sometimes Bernice would wake in the grip of some nameless alarm, run up the stairs in her nightgown and eyebrowless, and drub our windows with her hands, when we were sitting quietly at supper with our mother. These disruptions of her sleep were not less resented because they were self-generated. But she loved us for our mother's sake.

Bernice took a week off from work so that she could lend us her car for a visit to Fingerbone. When she learned from Helen that her mother was living, she began to urge her to go home for a while, and Helen, to her great satisfaction, was finally persuaded. It proved to be a fateful journey. Helen took us through the mountains and across the desert and into the mountains again, and at last to the lake and over the bridge into town, left at the light onto Sycamore Street and straight for six blocks. She put our suitcases in the screened porch, which was populated by a cat and a matronly washing machine, and told us to wait quietly. Then she went back to the car and drove north almost to Tyler, where she sailed in Bernice's Ford from the top of a cliff named Whiskey Rock into the blackest depth of the lake.

They searched for her. Word was sent out a hundred miles in every direction to watch for a young woman in a car which I said was blue and Lucille said was green. Some boys who had been fishing and knew nothing about the search had come across her sitting cross-legged on the roof of the car, which had bogged down in the meadow between the road and the cliff. They said she was gazing at the lake and eating wild strawberries, which were prodigiously large and abundant that year. She asked them very pleasantly to help her push her car out of the mud, and they went so far as to put their blankets and coats under the wheels to facilitate her rescue. When they got the Ford back to the road she thanked them, gave them her purse, rolled down the rear windows, started the car, turned the wheel as far to the right as it would go, and roared swerving and sliding across the meadow until she sailed off the edge of the cliff.

My grandmother spent a number of days in her bedroom. She had an armchair and a footstool from the parlor placed

by the window that looked into the orchard, and she sat
there, food was brought to her there. She was not inclined
to move. She could hear, if not the particular words and
conversations, at least the voices of people in the kitchen,
the gentle and formal society of friends and mourners that
had established itself in her house to look after things. Her
friends were very old, and fond of white cake and pinochle.
In twos and threes they would volunteer to look after us,
while the others played cards at the breakfast table. We
would be walked around by nervous, peremptory old men
who would show us Spanish coins, and watches, and
miniature jackknives with numerous blades designed to be
serviceable in any extremity, in order to keep us near them
and out of the path of possible traffic. A tiny old lady named
Ettie, whose flesh was the color of toadstools and whose
memory was so eroded as to make her incapable of bidding,
and who sat smiling by herself in the porch, took me by the
hand once and told me that in San Francisco, before the
fire, she had lived near a cathedral, and in the house
opposite lived a Catholic lady who kept a huge parrot on her
balcony. When the bells rang the lady would come out with
a shawl over her head and she would pray, and the parrot
would pray with her, the woman's voice and the parrot's
voice, on and on, between clamor and clangor. After a
while the woman fell ill, or at least stopped coming out on
her balcony, but the parrot was still there, and it whistled
and prayed and flirted its tail whenever the bells rang. The
fire took the church and its bells and no doubt the parrot,
too, and quite possibly the Catholic lady. Ettie waved it all
away with her hand and pretended to sleep.

For five years my grandmother cared for us very well. She
cared for us like someone reliving a long day in a dream.
Though she seemed abstracted, I think that, like one
dreaming, she felt more than the urgency of present
business, her attention heightened and at the same time

baffled by an awareness that this present had passed already, and had had its consequence. Indeed, it must have seemed to her that she had returned to relive this day because it was here that something had been lost or forgotten. She whited shoes and braided hair and fried chicken and turned back bedclothes, and then suddenly feared and remembered that the children had somehow disappeared, every one. How had it happened? How might she have known? And she whited shoes and braided hair and turned back bedclothes as if re-enacting the commonplace would make it merely commonplace again, or as if she could find the chink, the flaw, in her serenely orderly and ordinary life, or discover at least some intimation that her three girls would disappear as absolutely as their father had done. So when she seemed distracted or absent-minded, it was in fact, I think, that she was aware of too many things, having no principle for selecting the more from the less important, and that her awareness could never be diminished, since it was among the things she had thought of as familiar that this disaster had taken shape.

And it must have seemed, too, that she had only the frailest and most inappropriate tools for the most urgent uses. Once, she told us, she dreamed that she had seen a baby fall from an airplane and had tried to catch it in her apron, and once that she had tried to fish a baby out of a well with a tea strainer. Lucille and me she tended with scrupulous care and little confidence, as if her offerings of dimes and chocolate-chip cookies might keep us, our spirits, here in her kitchen, though she knew they might not. Her mother, she told us, knew a woman who, when she looked out her window at night, often saw the ghosts of children crying by the road. These children, who were sky black and stark naked and who danced with the cold and wiped their tears with the backs of their hands and the heels of their hands, furious with hunger, consumed much of the

woman's substance and most of her thoughts. She put out
soup, which the dogs ate, and blankets, which in the
morning were dewy and undisturbed. The children sucked
their fingers and hugged their sides as before, but she
thought she might have pleased them in some way because
they grew more numerous and came more often. When her
sister mentioned that people thought it was strange to put
supper out every night for the dogs to eat, she replied quite
sensibly that anyone who saw those poor children would do
exactly the same thing. Sometimes it seemed to me my
grandmother saw our black souls dancing in the moonless
cold and offered us deep-dish apple pie as a gesture of
well-meaning and despair.

And she was old. My grandmother was not a woman
given to excesses of any kind, and so her aging, as it became
advanced, was rather astonishing. True, she was straight
and brisk and bright when most of her friends had bobbling
heads or blurred speech or had sunk into wheelchairs or
beds. But in the last years she continued to settle and began
to shrink. Her mouth bowed forward and her brow sloped
back, and her skull shone pink and speckled within a mere
haze of hair, which hovered about her head like the
remembered shape of an altered thing. She looked as if the
nimbus of humanity were fading away and she were turning
monkey. Tendrils grew from her eyebrows and coarse white
hairs sprouted on her lip and chin. When she put on an old
dress the bosom hung empty and the hem swept the floor.
Old hats fell down over her eyes. Sometimes she put her
hand over her mouth and laughed, her eyes closed and her
shoulders shaking. In my earliest memories of her my
grandmother was already up in years. I remember sitting
under the ironing board, which pulled down from the
kitchen wall, while she ironed the parlor curtains and
muttered "Robin Adair." One veil after another fell down
around me, starched and white and fragrant, and I had

vague dreams of being hidden or cloistered, and watched the electric cord wag, and contemplated my grandmother's big black shoes, and her legs in their orangy-brown stockings, as contourless, as completely unshaped by muscle as two thick bones. Even then she was old.

Since my grandmother had a little income and owned her house outright, she always took some satisfaction in thinking ahead to the time when her simple private destiny would intersect with the great public processes of law and finance—that is, to the time of her death. All the habits and patterns and properties that had settled around her, the monthly checks from the bank, the house she had lived in since she came to it as a bride, the weedy orchard that surrounded the yard on three sides where smaller and wormier apples and apricots and plums had fallen every year of her widowhood, all these things would suddenly become liquid, capable of assuming new forms. And all of it would be Lucille's and mine.

"Sell the orchards," she would say, looking grave and wise, "but keep the house. So long as you look after your health, and own the roof above your head, you're as safe as anyone can be," she would say, "God willing." My grandmother loved to talk about these things. When she did, her eyes would roam over the goods she had accumulated unthinkingly and maintained out of habit as eagerly as if she had come to reclaim them.

Her sisters-in-law, Nona and Lily, were to come and look after us when the time came. Lily and Nona were twelve and ten years younger than my grandmother, and old as she was, she continued to think of them as rather young. They were almost destitute, and the savings in rent, not to mention the advantages of exchanging a little hotel room below ground for a rambling house surrounded by peonies and rose bushes, would be inducement enough to keep them with us until we came of age.

2

When, after almost five years, my grandmother one winter morning eschewed awakening, Lily and Nona were fetched from Spokane and took up housekeeping in Fingerbone, just as my grandmother had wished. Their alarm was evident from the first, in the nervous flutter with which they searched their bags and pockets for the little present they had brought (it was a large box of cough drops—a confection they considered both tasty and salubrious). Lily and Nona both had light blue hair and black coats with shiny black beads in intricate patterns on the lapels. Their thick bodies pitched forward from the hips, and their arms and ankles were plump. They were, though maiden ladies, of a buxomly maternal appearance that contrasted oddly with their brusque, unpracticed pats and kisses.

After their bags had been brought in, and they had kissed and patted us, Lily poked up the fire and Nona lowered the shades. Lily carried some of the larger bouquets into the porch and Nona poured more water into the vases. Then they seemed at a loss. I heard Lily remark to Nona that it was still three hours till suppertime, and five till bedtime. They eyed us with nervous sorrow. They found some *Reader's Digests* to read while we played go fish on the rug by the stove. A long hour passed and they gave us supper. Another hour and they put us to bed. We lay listening to their conversation, which was always perfectly audible, because they were both hard of hearing. It seemed then and always to be the elaboration and ornamentation of the consensus between them, which was as intricate and well-tended as a termite castle.

"A pity!"

"A pity, a pity!"

"Sylvia wasn't old."

"She wasn't young."

"She was old to be looking after children."

"She was young to pass away."

"Seventy-six?"

"Was she seventy-six?"

"That's not old."

"No."

"Not old for her family."

"I remember her mother."

"Spry as a girl at eighty-eight."

"But Sylvia had a harder life."

"Much harder."

"Much harder."

"Those daughters."

"How could things have gone so badly?"

"She wondered herself."

"Anyone would wonder."

"I know *I* would."

"That Helen!"

"Well, what about the little one, Sylvie?"

There was a clucking of tongues.

"At least she doesn't have children."

"So far as we know, at least."

"An itinerant."

"A migrant worker."

"A drifter."

There was a silence.

"She ought to be told about her mother."

"She should."

"If we could figure out where to find her."

"The ads in the papers might help."

"But I doubt it."

"I doubt it."

There was another silence.

"These two little girls."

"How could their mother have left them like that?"

"No note."

"No note was ever found."

"It couldn't have been an accident."

"It wasn't."

"That poor lady who lent her the car."

"I felt sorry for her."

"She blamed herself."

Someone got up from the table and put wood in the fire.

"They seem to be nice children."

"Very quiet."

"Not as pretty as Helen was."

"The one has pretty hair."

"They're not unattractive."

"Appearance isn't so important."

"More important for girls, of course."

"And they'll have to get along on their own."

"Poor things."

"Poor things."

"I'm glad they're quiet."

"The Hartwick was always so quiet."

"It was."

"It certainly was."

When they had gone to bed Lucille and I got up and sat by the window wrapped in a quilt and watched the few clouds fly. There was a bright moon in a storm ring, and Lucille made plans to build a moon dial out of snow under our window. The light at the window was strong enough to play cards by, but we could not read. We stayed awake the whole night because Lucille was afraid of her dreams.

Lily and Nona stayed with us during the depth of that winter. They were not in the habit of cooking. They complained of arthritis. My grandmother's friends invited them for pinochle, but they had never learned to play. They would not sing in a church choir because their voices had cracked. Lily and Nona, I think, enjoyed nothing except habit and familiarity, the precise replication of one day in the next. This was not to be achieved in Fingerbone, where any acquaintance was perforce new and therefore more objectionable than solitude, and where Lucille and I perpetually threatened to cough or outgrow our shoes.

It was a hard winter, too. The snow crested, finally, far above our heads. It drifted up our eaves on one side of the house. Some houses in Fingerbone simply fell from the weight of snow on their roofs, a source of grave and perpetual anxiety to my great-aunts, who were accustomed to a brick building, and to living below ground. Sometimes the sun would be warm enough to send a thick sheet of snow sliding off the roof, and sometimes the fir trees would shrug, and the snow would fall with surprisingly loud and earthy thuds, which would terrify my great-aunts. It was by grace of this dark and devastating weather that we were able to go very often to the lake to skate, for Lily and Nona knew that our house would fall, and hoped that we at least might be spared when it did, if only to die of pneumonia.

For some reason the lake was a source of particular pleasure to Fingerbone that year. It was frozen solid early and long. Several acres of it were swept, for people brought brooms to tend and expand it, till the cleared ice spread far across the lake. Sledders heaped snow on the shore into a precipitous chute that sent them sailing far across the ice. There were barrels on the shore for fires to be built in, and people brought boxes to sit on and planks and burlap bags to stand on around the barrels, and frankfurters to roast, and clothespins to clip frozen mittens to the lips of the barrels. A number of dogs began to spend most of their time at the ice. They were young, leggy dogs, affable and proprietary, and exhilarated by the weather. They liked to play at retrieving bits of ice which sped fantastically fast and far across the lake. The dogs made a gallant and youthful joke of their own strength and speed, and flaunted an utter indifference to the safety of their limbs. Lucille and I took our skates to school, so that we could go to the lake directly and stay there through the twilight. Usually we would skate along the edge of the swept ice, tracing its shape, and coming finally to its farthest edge, we would sit on the snow and look back at Fingerbone.

We felt giddily far from shore, though the lake was so solid that winter that it would certainly have supported the weight of the entire population of Fingerbone, past, present, and to come. Nevertheless, only we and the ice sweepers went out so far, and only we stayed.

The town itself seemed a negligible thing from such a distance. Were it not for the clutter on the shore, the flames and the tremulous pillars of heat that stood above the barrels, and of course the skaters who swooped and sailed and made bright, brave sounds, it would have been possible not to notice the town at all. The mountains that stood up behind it were covered with snow and hidden in the white sky, and the lake was sealed and hidden, yet their eclipse had not made the town more prominent. Indeed, where we were we could feel the reach of the lake far behind us, and far beyond us on either side, in a spacious silence that seemed to ring like glass. Lucille and I worked that winter on skating backward, and pivoting on one foot. We were often the last to leave, so absorbed we were in our skating and in the silence and the numbing sweetness of the air. The dogs would run out to us, rowdy and obstreperous, overjoyed that not everyone had left yet, and they would nip at our mittens and run circles around us so that we had no choice but to leave. And as we glided across the ice toward Fingerbone, we would become aware of the darkness, too close to us, like a presence in a dream. The comfortable yellow lights of the town were then the only comfort there was in the world, and there were not many of them. If every house in Fingerbone were to fall before our eyes, snuffing every light, the event would touch our senses as softly as a shifting among embers, and then the bitter darkness would step nearer.

We would find our boots and pull off our skates, and the dogs, excited by our haste, would put their muzzles in our faces and lick our mouths and run off with our scarves. "Ah, I hate those dogs," Lucille would say, and throw snowballs after them, which they chased with increasingly raucous delight and shattered in their teeth. They would even follow us home. We walked the blocks from the lake to our grandmother's house, jealous to the point of rage of those who were already accustomed to the light and the somnolent warmth of the houses we passed. The dogs shoved their muzzles into our hands and romped around us, nipping at our coats. When we finally came to our house, which was low and set back and apart by its orchard, we were not much surprised to see it still standing, the porch and kitchen lights shining as warmly as any we had passed. We pulled our boots off in the porch, smelling the warmth of the kitchen, and limped into the kitchen in our socks with our hands and feet and faces aching, where our aunts sat flushed by the vapors that rose from their stewing of chicken and baking of apples.

They smiled nervously at us and looked at each other. "This is much too late for little girls to come in!" Lily ventured, smiling at Nona. They watched us tensely and timidly, to see the result of their reprimand.

"The time went by so fast," Lucille said. "We're really sorry."

"You see, we can't go out looking for you."

"How could we find you?"

"We might get lost, or fall down on the road."

"The wind here is terrible, and there are no streetlights. They never sand the roads."

"Dogs are not on chains."

"And the cold is so bitter."

"It could freeze the life out of us. We feel it even in the house."

"We won't come back after dark any more," I said.

But since Lily and Nona were not really angry, they could not really be mollified. They felt only alarm. Here we were, cheeks flushed and eyes bright, already febrile, or lethally chilled, but, it may be, destined that night to plunge dreaming to the cellar floor, where we would lie under tons of snow and planks and shingles while above us neighbors scavenged in the ruins for kindling. And granting that this and even subsequent winters might spare us, there were still the perils of adolescence, of marriage, of childbirth, all formidable in themselves, but how many times compounded by our strange history?

Lily and Nona considered our prospects, and were baffled. Their appetites suffered, and so did their sleep. That particular evening a blizzard of remarkable ferocity blew up while we were eating our supper, and continued for four days. Lily was ladling stewed chicken over our biscuits when a limb from the apple orchard flew against the side of the house, and not ten minutes later a cable snapped somewhere, or a pole fell, and all of Fingerbone was plunged in darkness. It was not an unusual thing. Every pantry in town had in it a box of thick candles, the color of homemade soap, for use at such times. But my aunts grew silent, and watched each other. That night when we went to bed (with Vicks on strips of flannel pinned round our throats) they sat by the stove, turning over and over the fact that the Hartwick Hotel had never been known to accept a child, even for a single night.

"It would be lovely to take them home."

"They'd be safer."

"Warmer."

They clicked their tongues.

"We'd all be more comfortable."

"So near the hospital."

"That's an advantage, with children."

"I'm sure they'd be quiet."

"They're very quiet."

"Girls always are."

"Sylvia's were."

"Yes, they were."

After a moment, someone poked up the fire.

"We'd have help."

"Some advice."

"That Lottie Donahue could help. Her children are all right."

"I met the son once."

"Yes, so you said."

"He had an odd look. Always blinking. His nails were chewed down past the quick."

"Oh, I remember. He was awaiting trial for something."

"I don't remember just what."

"His mother never said."

Someone filled the teapot.

"Children are hard."

"For anybody."

"The Hartwick has always kept them out."

"And I understand that."

"I don't blame them."

"No."

"No."

They were quiet, stirring their tea.

"If we were Helen's age . . ."

". . . or Sylvie's."

"Or Sylvie's."

Again they were quiet.

"Young people understand them better."

"They don't worry so much."

"They're still almost children themselves."

"That's the truth. They haven't seen enough to worry like we do."

"It's as well."

"It's better."

"I think it *is* better."

"They enjoy children, I think."

"That's better for the children."

"In the short run."

"We think too much about the long run."

"And for all we know the house could fall tonight."

They were silent.

"I wish we would hear from Sylvie."

"Or at least hear *about* her."

"No one has seen her for years."

"Not in Fingerbone."

"She might have changed."

"No doubt she has."

"Improved."

"It's possible. People do."

"It's possible."

"Yes."

"Perhaps some attention from her family . . ."

"A family can help."

"Responsibility might help."

The spoons went round and round in the cups until someone finally said, " . . . a sense of home."

"It would be home to her."

"Yes, it would."

"It would."

So it must have seemed like providence when a note arrived from Sylvie herself. It was written in a large, elegant hand on a piece of pulpy tablet paper, torn neatly down one side and across the bottom, perhaps to correct the disproportion between the paper and the message, for she said only:

> Dear Mother, I may still be reached c/o Lost Hills Hotel, Billings, Montana. Write soon. I hope you are well. S.

Lily and Nona had composed a message to the effect that anyone knowing where Sylvia Fisher could be reached was asked to send the information to . . . and my grandmother's address. All other versions of the message amounted to announcements of my grandmother's death, and my aunts could not allow Sylvie to learn such a thing from the personal-ads section of a newspaper. They disliked newspapers, and were chagrined that anything touching themselves or their family should appear in them. It disturbed them enough that the actual obituary had already been bunched, no doubt, to cushion Christmas ornaments for storage, and spindled to start kitchen fires, though it was quite impressive and much admired. For my grandmother's passing had brought to mind the disaster that had widowed her. The derailment, though too bizarre in itself to have either significance or consequence, was nevertheless the most striking event in the town's history, and as such was prized. Those who were in any way associated with it were somewhat revered. Therefore, my grandmother's death occasioned a black-bordered page in the *Dispatch*, featuring photos of the train taken the day it was added to the line, and of workers hanging the bridge with crepe and wreaths, and of, in a row of gentlemen, a man identified as my grandfather. All the men in the photo wore high collars and hair combed flat across their brows. My grandfather had his lips a little parted and looked at the camera a little sidelong, and his expression seemed to be one of astonishment. There was no picture of my grandmother. For that matter, the time of the funeral was not mentioned. Nona and Lily speculated that if some vagary of wind should carry this black-bordered page under Sylvie's eyes, she might not know that her own mother's death had occasioned this opening of the town's slender archives, though the page might itself seem portentous, like an opening of graves.

Despite the omission of even essential information about my grandmother ("They wouldn't want to mention Helen," Lily speculated *sotto voce*, as she judged such things), it was considered an impressive tribute to her and was expected to be a source of pride to us. I was simply alarmed. It suggested to me that the earth had opened. In fact, I dreamed that I was walking across the ice on the lake, which was breaking up as it does in the spring, softening and shifting and pulling itself apart. But in the dream the surface that I walked on proved to be knit up of hands and arms and upturned faces that shifted and quickened as I stepped, sinking only for a moment into lower relief under my weight. The dream and the obituary together created in my mind the conviction that my grandmother had entered into some other element upon which our lives floated as weightless, intangible, immiscible, and inseparable as re- flections in water. So she was borne to the depths, my grandmother, into the undifferentiated past, and her comb had no more of the warmth of a hand about it than Helen of Troy's would have.

Even before Sylvie's note arrived, Lily and Nona had begun to compose a letter to inform her of her loss, and to invite her home to discuss the disposition and management of her mother's estate. My grandmother's will did not mention Sylvie. Her provisions for us did not include her in any way. This began to seem strange to Lily and Nona—if not unreasonable, then certainly unkind. They agreed that the forgiveness of the parent should always be extended to the erring child, even posthumously. So Lucille and I began to anticipate the appearance of our mother's sister with all the guilty hope that swelled our guardian's talcy bosoms. She would be our mother's age, and might amaze us with her resemblance to our mother. She would have grown up with our mother in this very house, and in the care of our grandmother. No doubt we had eaten the same casseroles, heard the same songs, and had our failings berated in the same terms. We began to hope, if unawares, that a substantial restitution was about to be made. And we overheard Lily and Nona in the kitchen at night, embroidering their hopes. Sylvie would be happy here. She knew the town—the dangerous places, the unsavory people—and could watch us, and warn us, as they could not. They began to consider it a failure of judgment, which they were reluctant to account for in terms of my grandmother's age, to prefer them over Sylvie. And we felt they must be right. All that could be said against Sylvie was that her mother omitted her name from virtually all conversation, and from her will. And while this was damaging, it gave neither us nor our great-aunts anything in particular to fear. Her itinerancy might be simple banishment. Her drifting, properly considered, might be no more than a preference for the single life, made awkward in her case by lack of money. Nona and Lily had stayed with their mother until she died,

and then moved west to be near their brother, and had lived
many years independently and alone on the money that
came from the sale of their mother's farm. If they had been
cast out and disinherited—they clucked their tongues—
"We'd have been riding around in freight cars, too." They
chortled in their bosoms and their chairs shifted. "It's only
the truth," one said, "that her mother had very little
patience with people who chose not to marry."

"She'd say as much."

"Before our faces."

"Many a time."

"God rest her."

We knew enough about Sylvie to know that she had
simply chosen not to act married, though she had a
marriage of sufficient legal standing to have changed her
name. No word had ever indicated who or what this Fisher
might have been. Lily and Nona chose not to bother about
him. Increasingly they saw in Sylvie a maiden lady, unlike
themselves only because she had been cast out unprovided
for. If they could find out where she was, they would invite
her. "Then we'll use our own judgment." After the note
arrived, they began to put their letter in final form, being
careful to suggest but not to promise that she might take her
mother's place in the household if she wished. Once the
letter was mailed, we all lived in a state of anticipation.
Lucille and I argued about whether her hair would be
brown or red. Lucille would say, "I know it'll be brown like
Mother's," and I'd reply, "Hers wasn't brown. It was red."

Lily and Nona conferred together and decided that they
must leave (for they had their health to consider, and they
longed to return to their basement room in the red-brick
and upright Hartwick Hotel, with its stiff linens and its
bright silver, where the arthritic bellhop and the two old
chambermaids deferred so pleasantly to their age and their
solitude and their poverty) and that Sylvie must come.

3

It was still late winter when they sent for her and it was not yet spring when she came. They had urged her to consider before she replied, and they had assured her at length and in the kindliest language (the letter was some days in composition) that there was no urgency in their request and that she must take all the time she needed to set her affairs in order before she came, if she should do so. And then one day as we sat at supper in the kitchen, and they worried between them about her not writing back, and remembered her as too dreaming and self-absorbed to be ordinarily considerate, and hoped she was not ill, Sylvie knocked at the door.

Nona went down to the door (the hall from the kitchen to the front door sloped rather sharply, though the angle was eased somewhat by a single step midway), rustling with all the slippery frictions of her old woman's clothing and underclothing. We heard her murmuring, "My dear! So cold! You walked? Come in the kitchen!" and then her rustling and her heavy shoes coming back up the hallway and not a sound more.

Sylvie came into the kitchen behind her, with a quiet that seemed compounded of gentleness and stealth and self-effacement. Sylvie was about thirty-five, tall, and narrowly built. She had wavy brown hair fastened behind her ears with pins, and as she stood there, she smoothed the stray hairs back, making herself neat for us. Her hair was wet, her hands were red and withered from the cold, her feet were bare except for loafers. Her raincoat was so shapeless and oversized that she must have found it on a bench. Lily and Nona glanced at each other, eyebrows raised. There was a little silence, and then Sylvie hesitantly put her icy hand on my head and said, "You're Ruthie. And you're Lucille. Lucille has the lovely red hair."

Lily stood up then and took both of Sylvie's hands, and Sylvie stooped to be kissed. "Here, sit here by the heater," she said, pushing a chair. Sylvie sat down.

"It's really warmest by the stove," said Nona. "Take your coat off, dear. You'll warm up faster. I'll poach an egg for you."

"Do you like poached eggs?" Lily asked. "I could boil one."

"Either way would be fine," Sylvie said. "A poached egg would be very nice." She unbuttoned her coat and slipped her arms out of the sleeves. "What a lovely dress!" Lily exclaimed. Sylvie smoothed her skirt with her long hands. The dress was a deep green, with a satiny shine. It had short sleeves and a large round collar on which there was a brooch, a little bunch of lilies of the valley. She looked at us all and looked down at her dress again, clearly pleased that it had made an impression. "Yes, you look very nice, my dear. Very well," Nona said, rather loudly. She really intended this observation for her sister, just as Lily's compliment had been intended for her. They shouted, for the sake of the other's comprehension and because neither of them could gauge her voice very well, and each of them considered her sister's hearing worse than her own, so each of them spoke a little louder than she had to. And they had lived all their lives together, and felt that they had a special language between them. So when Lily said, with a glance at Nona, "What a lovely dress," it was as if to say, "She seems rather sane! She seems rather normal!" And when Nona said, "You look very well," it was as if to say, "Perhaps she'll do! Perhaps she can stay and we can go!" Sylvie sat in the simple kitchen light with her hands in her lap and her eyes on her hands, while Lily and Nona stalked about on their stiff old legs, poaching eggs and dishing up stewed prunes, flushed and elated by their secret understanding.

"Did you know Mr. Simmons died?" Lily asked.

"He must have been very old," Sylvie said.

"And do you remember a Danny Rappaport?"

Sylvie shook her head.

"He was a class behind you in school."

"I guess I should remember him."

"Well, he died. I don't know how."

Nona said, "The funeral was announced in the paper, but there was no article about it. We thought that was strange. Just a photograph."

"Not recent, either," Lily grumbled. "He looked nineteen. Not a line in his face."

"Was Mother's funeral nice?" Sylvie asked.

"Lovely."

"Oh, yes, very nice."

The old sisters looked at each other.

"Very small, though, of course," Nona said.

"Yes, she wanted it small. But you should have seen the flowers! The whole house was full. We sent half of them over to the church."

"She didn't want flowers," Nona said. "She would have called it a waste."

"She didn't want a service."

"I see."

There was a silence. Nona buttered a piece of toast and slid the jelled egg onto it and broke it up with a fork as if it were for a child. Sylvie took a chair at the table and ate with her head on her hand. Nona went upstairs, and in a few minutes came down again, carrying a hot-water bottle. "I've put you in the hall bedroom. It's a little close, but that's better than a draft. There are two heavy blankets on the bed, and one lighter one, and I put a comforter on the chair." She filled the hot-water bottle with water from the kettle and bundled it in tea towels. Lucille and I each took a suitcase and followed Sylvie upstairs.

The stairs were wide and polished, with a heavy railing and spindle banisters, dating as they did from a time when my grandfather was growing confident enough of his carpentry to use good materials and to build things that might be considered permanent. But they terminated rather oddly in a hatch or trapdoor, because at the top of the stairs one came face to face with a wall so essential to supporting the roof (which had always sagged somewhat in the middle) that my grandfather could not bring himself to cut another door in it. So instead he had worked out a device with pulleys and window weights that made the trapdoor (which was left over from the time when the second floor was merely a loft with a ladder up to it) rise at the slightest push and then fall shut again of its own accord with a little slam. (This device prevented drafts from sweeping down the polished steps in torrents, flooding the parlor, eddying into the kitchen.) Sylvie's bedroom was really a sort of narrow dormer with a curtain closing it off from the hallway. There was a cot in it, fattened with pillows and blankets, and a little lamp, which Nona had left burning on a shelf. There was a single round window, small and high as a fully risen moon. The dresser and chair were outside the curtain, one on each side. Sylvie, in the half-dark hallway, turned and kissed each of us. "I'll get you presents," she whispered. "Tomorrow, maybe." She kissed us again and went behind the curtain, into the narrow room.

I have often wondered what it seemed like to Sylvie to come back to that house, which would have changed since she left it, shifted and settled. I imagine her with her grips in her bare hands, walking down the middle of the road, which was narrowed by the banks of plowed snow on either side, and narrowed more by the slushy pools that were forming at the foot of each bank. Sylvie always walked with her head down, to one side, with an abstracted and considering expression, as if someone were speaking to her in a soft voice. But she would have glanced up sometimes at the snow, which was the color of heavy clouds, and the sky, which was the color of melting snow, and all the slick black planks and sticks and stumps that erupted as the snow sank away.

How must it have seemed to step into the narrow hallway which still kept (as it seemed to me) a trace of the rude odor that the funeral flowers had begun to make before Nona could bring herself to throw them away. Her hands and feet must have ached from the warmth. I remember how red and twisted her hands looked, lying in the lap of her green dress, and how she pressed her arms to her sides. I remember that, as she sat there in a wooden chair in the white kitchen, smoothing her borrowed-looking dress and working her feet out of her loafers, sustaining all our stares with the placid modesty of a virgin who has conceived, her happiness was palpable.

The day after Sylvie arrived, Lucille and I woke up early. It was our custom to prowl the dawn of any significant day.

Ordinarily the house would belong to us for an hour or more, but that morning we found Sylvie sitting in the kitchen by the stove, with her coat on, eating oyster crackers from a small cellophane bag. She blinked at us, smiling. "It was nice with the light off," she suggested, and Lucille and I collided in our haste to pull the chain. Sylvie's coat made us think she might be leaving, and we were ready to perform great feats of docility to keep her. "Isn't that nicer?" In fact, the wind was badgering the house, throwing frozen rain against the windows. We sat down on the rug by her feet and watched her. She handed us each an oyster cracker. "I can hardly believe I'm here," she said finally. "I was on the train for eleven hours. There's so much snow in the mountains. We just crept along, for hours and hours and hours." It was clear from her voice that the trip had been pleasant. "Have you ever been on a train?" We had not. "They have heavy white tablecloths in the dining car, and little silver vases bolted to the window frame, and you get your own little silver pot of hot syrup. I like to travel by train," Sylvie said. "Especially in the passenger cars. I'll take you with me sometime."

"Take us where?" Lucille asked.

Sylvie shrugged. "Somewhere. Wherever. Where do you want to go?"

I saw the three of us posed in all the open doors of an endless train of freight cars—innumerable, rapid, identical images that produced a flickering illusion of both movement and stasis, as the pictures in a kinetoscope do. The hot and dangerous winds of our passing tattered the Queen Anne's lace, and yet, for all the noise and clatter and headlong speed, we flickered there at the foot of the garden while the train roared on and on. "Spokane," I said.

"Oh, somewhere better than that. Farther away. Maybe Seattle." There was a silence. "But that's where you used to live."

"With our mother," Lucille said.

"Yes." Sylvie had folded the empty cellophane wrapper in quarters and she was creasing the folds between finger and thumb.

"Would you tell us about her?" Lucille asked. The question was abrupt, and the tone of it was coaxing, because adults did not wish to speak to us about our mother. Our grandmother never spoke of any of her daughters, and when they were mentioned to her, she winced with irritation. We were accustomed to this, but not to the sharp embarrassment with which Lily and Nona and all my grandmother's friends reacted to our mother's very name. We had planned to try Sylvie, but perhaps because Sylvie had her coat on and appeared so very transient, Lucille did not wait till we knew her better, as we had agreed to do.

"Oh, she was nice," Sylvie said. "She was pretty."

"But what was she *like*?"

"She was good in school."

Lucille sighed.

"It's hard to describe someone you know so well. She was very quiet. She played the piano. She collected stamps." Sylvie seemed to be reflecting. "I've never known anyone so fond of cats. She was always bringing them home."

Lucille shifted her legs and adjusted the thick flannel skirt of her nightgown around them.

"I didn't see much of her after she was married," Sylvie explained.

"Then tell us about her wedding," Lucille said.

"Oh, that was very small. She wore a sundress made of eyelet lace, and a straw hat, and she had a bouquet of daisies. It was just to please Mother. They'd already been married by a justice of the peace somewhere in Nevada."

"Why Nevada?"

"Well, your father was from Nevada."

"What was he like?"

Sylvie shrugged. "He was tall. Not bad-looking. Awfully quiet, though. I think he was shy."

"What kind of work did he do?"

"He traveled. I think he sold some sort of farming equipment. Tools, maybe. I never even saw him, except for that one day. Do you know where he is now?"

"Nope," I said. Lucille and I were remembering a day when Bernice had brought our mother a thick letter. "Reginald Stone," she had said, tapping the return address with a lavender claw. Helen gave her a cup of coffee and sat at the table picking idly at a loose corner of the postage stamp while Bernice whispered a scandalous tale of marital fracture and reconciliation involving a cocktail waitress Bernice knew very well. Apparently concluding at last that the letter would never be opened while she was there, Bernice finally left, and when she was gone Helen tore the envelope into fourths and dropped them in the trash. Glancing into our faces as if she suddenly remembered we were there, anticipating our questions, she said, "It's best," and that was all we knew of our father.

I could conjure her face as it was then, startled by the sudden awareness of our watching. At the time I think I felt only curiosity, though I suppose I remember that glance because she looked at me for signs of more than curiosity. And, in fact, I recall the moment now with some astonishment—there was neither doubt nor passion in her destruction of the letter, neither hesitation nor haste—and with frustration—there was only that letter and never another one, and nothing else from him or about him at all—and with anger—he was presumably our father, and might wish to know what had become of us, and even to intervene. It occurs to me sometimes that as I grow older I am increasingly able to present to her gaze the face she seemed to expect. But of course she was looking into a face I do not remember—no more like mine than Sylvie's is like hers. Less like, perhaps, because, as I watched Sylvie, she reminded me of my mother more and more. There was such similarity, in fact, in the structure of cheek and chin, and the texture of hair, that Sylvie began to blur the memory of my mother, and then to displace it. Soon it was Sylvie who would look up startled, regarding me from a vantage of memory in which she had no place. And it was increasingly to this remembered Sylvie that I presented my look of conscious injury, knowing as I did so that Sylvie could know nothing of that letter.

What did Sylvie see when she thought of my mother? A girl with braided hair, a girl with freckled arms, who liked to lie on the rug in the lamplight, flat on her belly with her heels in the air and her chin on her two fists, reading Kipling. Did she tell lies? Could she keep secrets? Did she tickle, or slap, or pinch, or punch, or grimace? If someone had asked me about Lucille I would remember her with her mass of soft, fine, tangly hair concealing ears that cupped a bit and grew painfully cold if she did not cover them. I would remember that her front teeth, the permanent ones, came in, first one and much later the other, immense and raggedly serrated, and that she was fastidious about washing her hands. I would remember that when irked she bit her lip, when shy she scratched her knee, that she smelled dully clean, like chalk, or like a sun-warmed cat.

I do not think Sylvie was merely reticent. It is, as she said, difficult to describe someone, since memories are by their nature fragmented, isolated, and arbitrary as glimpses one has at night through lighted windows. Sometimes we used to watch trains passing in the dark afternoon, creeping through the blue snow with their windows all alight, and full of people eating and arguing and reading newspapers. They could not see us watching, of course, because by five-thirty on a winter day the landscape had disappeared, and they would have seen their own depthless images on the black glass, if they had looked, and not the black trees and the black houses, or the slender black bridge and the dim blue expanse of the lake. Some of them probably did not know what it was the train approached so cautiously. Once, Lucille and I walked beside the train to the shore. There had been a freezing rain that glazed the snow with a crust of ice, and we found that, when the sun went down, the crust was thick enough for us to walk on. So we followed the train at a distance of twenty feet or so, falling now and then, because the glazed snow swelled and sank in dunes, and the tops of bushes and fence posts rose out of it in places where we did not expect them to be. But by crawling up, and sliding down, and steadying ourselves against the roofs of sheds and rabbit hutches, we managed to stay just abreast of the window of a young woman with a small head and a small hat and a brightly painted face. She wore pearl-gray gloves that reached almost to her elbows, and hooped bracelets that fell down her arms when she reached up to push a loose wisp of hair underneath her hat. The woman looked at the window very often, clearly absorbed by what she saw, which was not but merely seemed to be Lucille and me scrambling to stay beside her, too breathless to shout. When we came to the shore, where the land fell down and the bridge began to rise, we stopped and watched her window sail slowly away, along the abstract arc of the bridge. "We could walk across the lake," I said. The thought was terrible. "It's too cold," Lucille replied. So she was gone. Yet I remember her neither less nor differently than I remember others I have known better, and indeed I dream of her, and the dream is very like the event itself, except that in the dream the bridge pilings do not tremble so perilously under the weight of the train.

"What would you like for breakfast?" Sylvie asked.

"Cornflakes."

She made cocoa and we ate and watched the day come.

It had been a cold night that froze the slush and hardened
the heaps of dirty, desiccated snow by the sides of the road.
"I'm going to take a little walk around town," Sylvie said.
"Before the roads all turn to mud again. I'll be back soon."
She buttoned her coat and stepped out into the porch. We
heard the screen door slam. "She should have borrowed a
scarf," I said. "She isn't coming back," Lucille replied. We
ran upstairs and put on our jeans, stuffing the skirts of our
nightgowns into them. We pulled our boots on over our
bedroom slippers and grabbed our coats and ran outside,
but she was gone already. If she was leaving, she would go
into town, to the station. If she was not leaving, she would
probably go to town anyway, unless she went to the lake.
Since she was bareheaded, and had neither gloves nor
boots, the shore would be miserably difficult and cold. We
walked toward Main Street as fast as we could over the
frozen slush and the frozen ruts and shards of ice. "I bet Lily
and Nona told her to leave," I said. Lucille shook her head.
Her face was flushed and her cheeks were wet. "It'll be all
right," I said. She wiped her face roughly with her sleeve.
"I know it'll be all right, but it makes me mad."
    We turned the corner and saw Sylvie in the road ahead of
us, chucking chunks of ice at four or five dogs. She would
pick up a bit of ice and toss it from hand to hand, walking
backward, while the dogs followed after her and circled
behind her, yapping. We saw her pelt one squat mongrel in
the ribs, and all the dogs scattered. She sucked her fingers
and blew into her cupped hands, and then picked up
another piece of ice just as the dogs came back and began
yapping and circling again. Her manner was insouciant and
her aim was deft. She did not notice us standing at a
distance watching her. We stood where we were until the
last of the dogs turned and trotted back to its porch, and
then we followed her at a distance of two blocks into
downtown Fingerbone. She walked slowly past the drug-

store and the dime store and the dry-goods store, stopping to look into each of the windows. Then she walked directly to the railroad station and went inside. Lucille and I walked down to the station. We could see her standing by the stove, with her arms folded, studying the chalked list of arrivals and departures. Lucille said, "I'm going to tell her she forgot her bags." I had not thought of that. When Sylvie saw us coming in she smiled with surprise. "You left your stuff at our house," Lucille said.

"Oh, I just came in here to get warm. Nothing else is open. It's early, you know. I forgot how early the sun rises these days." She rubbed her hands together in the warmth of the stove. "It still *feels* like winter, doesn't it?"

"Why don't you wear gloves?" Lucille asked.

"I left them on the train."

"Why don't you wear boots?"

Sylvie smiled. "I suppose I should."

"You also need a hat. You should use hand lotion."

Sylvie put her hands in her pockets. "I think I should stay for a while," she said. "The aunts are too old. I think it's best for now, at least."

Lucille nodded.

"We'll get some pie when the café opens. And then you can help me choose a scarf, and maybe some gloves." She groped in her pockets and brought out a little ball of paper money and some change. She looked at the money doubtfully and did not count it. "We'll see."

"We have hand lotion at home," Lucille replied.

At nine o'clock we followed Sylvie to the five-and-ten, where she bought a plaid scarf and gray gloves. It took her some time to choose them, and some time to explain who she was to the woman at the cash register, who, though Sylvie thought she looked familiar, was new in town and knew nothing of our family. When we came back into the street the sun was shining warmly. There was a bright flow

of water in the gutters. When we came to the end of the
sidewalk, there was no way for Sylvie to walk without now
and then stepping over her shoes in water of one sort or
another. This difficulty seemed to absorb her but not to
disturb her.

"That woman reminded me of someone, but I can't think
who," Sylvie said.

"Do you still have friends here?" Lucille asked.

Sylvie laughed. "Well, the fact is, I never did have many
friends here. We kept to ourselves. We knew who everyone
was, that's all. And now I've been away—sixteen years."

"But you came back sometimes," Lucille said.

"No."

"Where were you married?" Lucille asked.

"Here."

"Then that's once."

"Once," Sylvie said.

Lucille squashed a lump of slush with her boot, and I
slapped her because some of it flew against my leg.

We went up the walk to our porch. Lily and Nona were
in the kitchen, rosy with warmth and perturbation.

"Here you are!" Lily said.

"What a day to go walking!"

Sylvie had pried off her sodden loafers in the porch, and
we had pulled off our coats and boots. The aunts clucked
their tongues when they saw us in our jeans and slippers,
and still in our nightgowns with our hair uncombed. "Ah!"
they said. "What is this?"

Lucille said, "Ruthie and I woke up early this morning,
and we decided to go outside to see the sun come up. We
went clear downtown. Sylvie was worried, so she came out
looking for us."

"Oh, I'm surprised at you girls," Nona said.

"Such a thoughtless thing to do."

"I hope Sylvie gave you a good talking-to."

"Poor Sylvie!"

"If we'd been here by ourselves, we'd have died of worry."

"We *would* have."

"The roads are so treacherous. What would we have done?"

They brought Sylvie a cup of coffee and a pan of hot water for her feet, clucking and commiserating and patting her hands and her hair.

"You have to be young to deal with children!"

"That's a fact."

"We'd have had to get the sheriff."

"It might have taught them a lesson."

The aunts hurried away to finish packing. Lucille opened the newspaper to the crossword puzzle, and found a pencil in a drawer, and sat down across the table from Sylvie.

"The element represented by the symbol Fe," she said. Sylvie answered, "Iron."

"Wouldn't it start with F?"

"It's iron," Sylvie said. "They try to trick you."

That evening Lily and Nona were taken by a friend of my grandmother's back to Spokane and we and the house were Sylvie's.

4

The week after Sylvie arrived, Fingerbone had three days of brilliant sunshine and four of balmy rain. On the first day the icicles dripped so rapidly that the gravel under the eaves rattled and jumped. The snow was granular in the shade, and in the sun it turned soft and clung damply to whatever it covered. The second day the icicles fell and broke on the ground and snow drooped low over the eaves in a heavy mass. Lucille and I poked it down with sticks. The third day the snow was so dense and malleable that we made a sort of statue. We put one big ball of snow on top of another, and carved them down with kitchen spoons till we had made a figure of a woman in a long dress, her arms folded. It was Lucille's idea that she should look to the side, and while I knelt and whittled folds into her skirt, Lucille stood on the kitchen stool and molded her chin and her nose and her hair. It happened that I swept her skirt a little back from her hip, and that her arms were folded high on her breasts. It was mere accident—the snow was firmer here and softer there, and in some places we had to pat clean snow over old black leaves that had been rolled up into the snowballs we made her from—but her shape became a posture. And while in any particular she seemed crude and lopsided, altogether her figure suggested a woman standing in a cold wind. It seemed that we had conjured a presence. We took off our coats and hats and worked about her in silence. That was the third day of sunshine. The sky was dark blue, there was no wind at all, but everywhere an audible seep and trickle of melting. We hoped the lady would stand long enough to freeze, but in fact while we were stamping the gray snow all smooth around her, her head pitched over and smashed on the ground. This accident cost her a forearm and a breast. We made a new snowball for a head, but it crushed her eaten neck, and under the weight of it a shoulder dropped away. We went inside for lunch, and when we came out again, she was a dog-yellowed stump in which neither of us would admit any interest.

Days of rain at just that time were a disaster. They hastened the melting of the snow but not the thawing of the ground. So at the end of three days the houses and hutches and barns and sheds of Fingerbone were like so many spilled and foundered arks. There were chickens roosting in the telephone poles and dogs swimming by in the streets. My grandmother always boasted that the floods never reached our house, but that spring, water poured over the thresholds and covered the floor to the depth of four inches, obliging us to wear boots while we did the cooking and washing up. We lived on the second floor for a number of days. Sylvie played solitaire on the vanity while Lucille and I played Monopoly on the bed. The firewood on the porch was piled high so that most of it stayed dry enough to burn, though rather smokily. The woodpile was full of spiders and mice, and the pantry curtain rod was deeply bowed by the weight of water climbing up the curtains. If we opened or closed a door, a wave swept through the house, and chairs tottered, and bottles and pots clinked and clunked in the bottoms of the kitchen cabinets.

After four days of rain the sun appeared in a white sky, febrile and dazzling, and the people who had left for higher ground came back in rowboats. From our bedroom window we could see them patting their roofs and peering in at their attic windows. "I have never seen such a thing," Sylvie said. The water shone more brilliantly than the sky, and while we watched, a tall elm tree fell slowly across the road. From crown to root, half of it vanished in the brilliant light.

Fingerbone was never an impressive town. It was chastened by an outsized landscape and extravagant weather, and chastened again by an awareness that the whole of human history had occurred elsewhere. That flood flattened scores of headstones. More disturbing, the graves sank when the water receded, so that they looked a little like hollow sides or empty bellies. And then the library was flooded to a depth of three shelves, creating vast gaps in the Dewey decimal system. The losses in hooked and braided rugs and needlepoint footstools will never be reckoned. Fungus and mold crept into wedding dresses and photograph albums, so that the leather crumbled in our hands when we lifted the covers, and the sharp smell that rose when we opened them was as insinuating as the smells one finds under a plank or a rock. Much of what Fingerbone had hoarded up was defaced or destroyed outright, but perhaps because the hoard was not much to begin with, the loss was not overwhelming.

The next day was very fine. The water was so calm that the sunken half of the fallen tree was replaced by the mirrored image of the half trunk and limbs that remained above the water. All day two cats prowled in the branches,

pawing at little eddies and currents. The water was beginning to slide away. We could hear the lake groan under the
weight of it, for the lake had not yet thawed. The ice would
still be thick, but it would be the color of paraffin, with big
white bubbles under it. In normal weather there would
have been perhaps an inch of water on top of it in shallow
places. Under all the weight of the flood water it sagged
and, being fibrous rather than soft or brittle, wrenched
apart, as resistant to breaching as green bones. The afternoon was loud with the giant miseries of the lake, and the
sun shone on, and the flood was the almost flawless mirror
of a cloudless sky, fat with brimming and very calm.

Lucille and I pulled on our boots and went downstairs.
The parlor was full of light. Our walking from the stairs to
the door had set off an intricate system of small currents
which rolled against the floorboards. Glyphs of crimped and
plaited light swung across the walls and the ceiling. The
couch and the armchairs were oddly dark. The stuffing in
their backs had slid, and the cushions had shallow craters in
the middles of them. Water seeped out when we touched
them. In the course of days the flood had made a sort of tea
of hemp and horsehair and rag paper in that room, a smell
which always afterward clung to it and which I remember
precisely at this minute, though I have never encountered
its like.

Sylvie came down the hall in a pair of my grandmother's
boots and looked in at us from the door. "Should we start
dinner?" she asked.

Lucille poked a sofa cushion with her finger. "Look," she
said. When she took her hand away, the suppurated water
vanished, but the dent remained.

"It's a shame," Sylvie said. From the lake came the
increasingly terrific sound of wrenching and ramming and
slamming and upending, as a south-flowing current heaped
huge shards of ice against the north side of the bridge.

Sylvie pushed at the water with the side of her foot. A ribbed
circle spread to the four walls and the curves of its four sides
rebounded, interpenetrating, and the orderly ranks of light
swept and swung about the room. Lucille stomped with her
feet until the water sloshed against the walls like water
carried in a bucket. There were the sounds of dull concus-
sion from the kitchen, and the lace curtains, drawn thin
and taut by their own sodden weight, shifted and turned.
Sylvie took me by the hands and pulled me after her
through six grand waltz steps. The house flowed around us.
Lucille pulled the front door open and the displacement she
caused made one end of the woodpile in the porch collapse
and tipped a chair, spilling a bag of clothespins. Lucille
stood at the door, looking out.

"It sounds like the bridge is breaking up," she remarked.

"That's probably just the ice," Sylvie said.

Lucille said, "I don't think Simmons's house is where it
used to be."

Sylvie went to the door and peered down the street at a
blackened roof. "It's so hard to tell."

"Those bushes used to be on the other side."

"Maybe the bushes have moved."

Sylvie and I started a smoldery fire and boiled water for
tea and soup, and Lucille piled up the fallen wood and
swept the bobbing clothespins behind the pantry curtain
with a broom (it was the same broom we used to whack the
woodpile before we used any wood from it, so that the
spiders and mice would be warned away, and would not bite
our fingers or drop into our sleeves, or perish in the stove
flames). Lily and Nona, in their alarm at leaving the house
to shop, and their fear of being snowed in or bedridden, had
arranged to have the pantry stocked with great quantities of
canned goods. We could have lived through a dozen floods
without difficulty. But it was disturbing to have our aunts'
fear appear as prescience.

We took our supper upstairs and sat on our bed and looked out over the town. It appeared to us that Simmons's house had indeed been lifted from its foundations. A breeze dulled the surface of the water as the sun descended amid a crying of stranded dogs and of one disoriented rooster. The clashes and groans from the lake continued unabated, dreadful at night, and the sound of the night wind in the mountains was like one long indrawn breath. Downstairs the flood bumped and fumbled like a blind man in a strange house, but outside it hissed and trickled, like the pressure of water against your eardrums, and like the sounds you hear in the moment before you faint.

Sylvie lit a candle. "Let's play crazy eights."

"I don't really want to," Lucille said.

"What do you want to do?"

"I want to find some other people."

"Now?"

"Well, tomorrow. We could just wade up to higher ground and walk around until we find someone. There must be a lot of people camping in the hills."

"But we're fine here," Sylvie said. "We can cook our own food and sleep in our own beds. What could be better?" She shuffled the cards and laid them out for solitaire.

"I'm very tired of it," Lucille said.

Sylvie picked up an ace and turned over the card beneath it. "It's the loneliness," Sylvie said. "Loneliness bothers lots of people. I knew a woman once who was so lonely she married an old man with a limp and had four children in five years, and none of it helped at all. Then she got the idea that she wanted to see her mother so she scraped up some money and drove all the way to Missouri with the children. She said her mother had changed so much that she wouldn't have recognized her on the street. The old woman took a look at the children and said she didn't see a trace of the family in them, and she said, 'You've stored up sorrow for yourself, Marie.' So she just turned around and went back home. But her husband would never believe it was her mother she had gone to see. He thought she had just left with the children and gotten scared of something and come back. He never really showed any of them much affection after that. But he didn't live long, anyway."

"What happened to the children?" Lucille asked.

Sylvie shrugged. "The usual things, I suppose. If there really were any children."

"I thought you said she had *four*."

"Well, I don't really know that she did. I just met her on the bus. She talked about everything under the sun, so I said, 'If you're getting off at Billings, I'll treat you to a hamburger.' She said, 'I'm not getting off at Billings.' But then she did. I was looking at some magazines I saw on a bench in the station, and I glanced up, and she was standing there not ten feet away, watching me. When I looked up, she turned around and ran out to the street and that's the last I saw of her. She was probably crazy. I thought at the time, 'She doesn't have children any more than I do.'"

"What made you think she didn't have children?"

"Well, if she did, I feel sorry for them. I knew a woman once who reminded me of her a lot. She had a little girl, and it was the saddest thing. She couldn't take her eyes off her. She wouldn't let her go outside, or play with other children. When the little girl fell asleep the woman would paint the little girl's nails and comb her hair into ringlets, and then she would wake her up to play with her, and if the little girl cried the woman cried, too. If the woman on the bus was as lonely as she said she was, she'd have her children with her. Unless she didn't have any children, or the court had taken them. That's what happened to the other little girl I was talking about."

"What court?" Lucille asked.

"A probate court. A judge, you know."

"Well, if a judge did take them, what would he do with them?"

"Oh, send them to some place. I think there's a farm or something."

That was the first Lucille or I had heard of the interest of the state in the well-being of children, and we were alarmed. By the light of the candle on the vanity, Sylvie flipped and sorted through her deck of cards, plainly unaware that the black shape of judicial attention stood over us all, as enormous as our shadows. Lucille and I still doubted that Sylvie would stay. She resembled our mother, and besides that, she seldom removed her coat, and every story she told had to do with a train or a bus station. But not till then did we dream that *we* might be taken from *her*. I imagined myself feigning sleep while Sylvie brushed my short brown hair into long golden ringlets, dropping each one carefully on the pillow. I imagined her seizing my hands and pulling me after her in a wild waltz down the hall, through the kitchen, through the orchard, the night moonless and I in my nightgown, almost asleep. Just when the water in the orchard had begun to rush from us and toward us and to leap against the trunks of trees and splash against our ankles, an old man in a black robe would step from behind a tree and take me by the hand—Sylvie too stricken to weep and I too startled to resist. Such a separation, I imagined, could indeed lead to loneliness intense enough to make one conspicuous in bus stations. It occurred to me that most people in bus stations would be conspicuous if it were not for the numbers of others there who would otherwise be conspicuous in the same way. Sylvie, at that moment, would hardly be noticed in a bus station.

"Why didn't you have children?" Lucille asked.

Sylvie lifted her shoulders. "It just wasn't in the cards," she said.

"Did you want them?"

"I always liked them."

"But, I mean, did you want to *have* them?"

"You must know, Lucille," Sylvie said, "that some questions aren't polite. I'm sure that my mother must have told you that."

"She's sorry," I said. Lucille bit her lip.

"It doesn't matter," Sylvie said. "Let's play crazy eights. I've got the deck warmed up."

We needed more chairs, and we needed to bring up the bricks that we heated on the top of the stove to hold in our laps and put under our feet, and to take down the bricks that had gone cold. Sylvie took the bricks down in a gunny sack and Lucille and I each carried a candle. When we got to the hall our candles went out. The trapdoor had been left open, admitting too strong a flow of air from below to permit a candle flame. Our matches died before we could even light the wicks. "Well," Sylvie said. She waded ahead of us to the kitchen. It was absolutely dark. We felt our way along the wall. When we came to the kitchen it was silent, except for the settling sounds of the low fire and the familiar, idle rummaging of the water in the depths of the pantry.

"Sylvie?"

"Here." Her voice came from the porch. "I'm just getting some wood. I've never seen such a dark night."

"Well, come back in!"

We heard the wash, wash, wash of her footsteps. "I really never have," she said. "It's like the end of the world!"

"Well, let's go back upstairs."

But Sylvie had fallen silent again. Guessing that she must be listening to something, we were silent, too. The lake still thundered and groaned, the flood waters still brimmed and simmered. When we did not move or speak, there was no proof that we were there at all. The wind and the water brought sounds intact from any imaginable distance. Deprived of all perspective and horizon, I found myself reduced to an intuition, and my sister and my aunt to something less than that. I was afraid to put out my hand, for fear it would touch nothing, or to speak, for fear no one would answer. We all stood there silently for a long moment.

Lucille said in a very loud voice, "I'm really tired of this."

Sylvie patted at my shoulder. "It's all right, Lucille."

"I'm not Lucille," I said.

Wash, wash, wash, Sylvie went to the stove. We heard her put the wood down on the drainboard, stack the cold bricks in the sink, put the hot bricks into the gunny sack. Then she took the handle and lifted a lid from the stove, and a dim, warm light shone on her face and hands and across the ceiling. She dropped in a stick. Embers burst and spilled and the light grew yellower and stronger. Sylvie added wood, a stick at a time, until flames leaped. We could see a miniature of the fire reflected in the window. The nickel fittings on the stove glowed red, and red lights bobbed on the flooded floor. Then she put the lid back on and the room was totally dark. "Remember the chairs," Sylvie said. We could hear her arranging the cold bricks on top of the stove. We groped our way to the stairs, each feeling the way with one hand and dragging a kitchen chair with the other. We worked the chairs through the trapdoor, leaving it open, found our room, closed the door, and lit a candle. For several minutes we heard only the usual watery sounds from below.

"I suppose she went out for another walk," Lucille said. But we both knew that she had fallen silent again in the dark.

"Let's call her," I said.

"Let's wait." Lucille sat down beside the vanity and dealt

us each seven cards. We played two indolent hands, and
still Sylvie did not appear.

"I'll call her," I said. When I opened the door, the candle
went out. I stood at the top of the stairs and shouted,
"Sylvie! Sylvie! Sylvie!" I thought I heard a shuffling, a
slight disarrangement of the water. I went back down the
stairs again, into the kitchen. I moved the bricks around on
top of the stove and opened the lid, releasing the light, but
the room was empty. I went out into the parlor, walking up
and down the room with my arms spread wide. Nothing.
"Sylvie!" I shouted, but there was no sound. I went back
through the kitchen and out to the porch, and there I
stumbled over some drifting firewood and fell to my knees.
I had to pull my boots off one at a time and empty them. No
one was there, either. No one was in the pantry. That left
my grandmother's room, which I dreaded entering because
it was three steps lower than the kitchen. "Sylvie?" I said.
"Why don't you come upstairs?"

There was a silence. "I will."

"Why not now? It's cold."

She did not reply. I started down the steps. After the
second, my boots were swamped again and I had to pull
them off. I walked, with my arms outstretched, in the
direction of her voice, and finally I brushed the canvassy
folds of her coat. She was leaning against the window, I
could see her barely silhouetted. I could feel the chill of the
glass. "Sylvie?" She stood still as an effigy. I reached into her
pocket and brought out a cold hand. I opened it and closed
it and rubbed it between my hands, but she did not move or
speak. I reached up and touched her cheek and her nose. A
nerve jumped in the lid of her eye, but she did not move.
Then I drew back my arm and hit her across the middle.
The blow landed among the folds of her coat with a dull
whump.

She laughed. "Why did you do that?"

"Well, why won't you talk?"

I began pulling her by her coat in the direction of the door. I continued to pull although she followed unresistingly, pausing only to lift down her bag of bricks from the dresser as we passed. I pulled her all the way up the stairs and through the bedroom door. Lucille stood bent over the candle with her hands cupped around the flame. Nevertheless it went out. "That was the last match," she said.

"It's your turn to go downstairs," I said. "Get a coal from the stove to light it with." Lucille went and stood on the stairs for a long time.

"I'll go, Lucille," Sylvie said.

Lucille almost ran down the stairs. We heard the slish and moil of her steps in the hall and kitchen, and the business at the stove. She came back upstairs holding a coal in a china cup. I held the wick against it and blew, and the room was light again. Sylvie walked over to the vanity. The cards were dealt for a third hand. "You started without me," she said. We put bricks on the floor for our feet and wrapped ourselves in quilts and played gin rummy.

During those days Fingerbone was strangely transformed. If one should be shown odd fragments arranged on a silver tray and be told, "That is a splinter from the True Cross, and that is a nail paring dropped by Barabbas, and that is a bit of lint from under the bed where Pilate's wife dreamed her dream," the very ordinariness of the things would recommend them. Every spirit passing through the world fingers the tangible and mars the mutable, and finally has come to look and not to buy. So shoes are worn and hassocks are sat upon and finally everything is left where it was and the spirit passes on, just as the wind in the orchard picks up the leaves from the ground as if there were no other pleasure in the world but brown leaves, as if it would deck, clothe, flesh itself in flourishes of dusty brown apple leaves, and then drops them all in a heap at the side of the house and goes on. So Fingerbone, or such relics of it as showed above the mirroring waters, seemed fragments of the quotidian held up to our wondering attention, offered somehow as proof of their own significance. But then suddenly the lake and the river broke open and the water slid away from the land, and Fingerbone was left stripped and blackened and warped and awash in mud.

The restoration of the town was an exemplary community effort in which we had no part. My grandmother had been rather isolated because she had no interest in people younger than herself. We and the paperboy were the only people under sixty to whom she was consistently polite. Lily and Nona, of course, had had little contact with local society, and Sylvie claimed not to know anybody in Fingerbone at all. Now and then she would say that someone on the street resembled So-and-so, was just the right height and the right age, but she was content simply to marvel at the resemblance. Then, too, for whatever reasons, our whole family was standoffish. This was the fairest description of our best qualities, and the kindest description of our worst faults. That we were self-sufficient, our house reminded us always. If its fenestration was random, if its corners were out of square, my grandfather had built it himself, knowing nothing whatever of carpentry. And he had had the good judgment to set it on a hill, so while others were pushing drowned mattresses out second-story windows, we simply spooled up our living-room rug and propped it on the porch steps. (The couch and chairs were imponderably heavy, so we stuffed rags under them and left them to drip for a week or so.) We had been assured by our elders that intelligence was a family trait. All my kin and forebears were people of substantial or remarkable intellect, though somehow none of them had prospered in the world. Too bookish, my grandmother said with tart pride, and

Lucille and I read constantly to forestall criticism, anticipating failure. If my family were not as intelligent as we
were pleased to pretend, this was an innocent deception, for
it was a matter of indifference to everybody whether we were
intelligent or not. People always interpreted our slightly
formal manner and our quiet tastes as a sign that we wished
to stay a little apart. This was a matter of indifference, also,
and we had our wish.

The neighbors satisfied themselves now that we were
alive, accepted with thanks a few cans of corn and succo-
tash, glanced with polite envy at the relative comfort and
order of our household ("I would ask you to sit down,"
Sylvie always explained, "but the couch is full of water"),
and slogged home again. An old gentleman came to our
door to ask for a slip of philodendron, since his had
drowned, and various women came to ask after cats and
dogs that they thought might have sheltered with us. Two
weeks after the water was gone people began to believe that
our house had not been touched by the flood at all.

5

After the mud had been shoveled away, school took up again. Fingerbone had a tall red-brick junior high school. It was named for William Henry Harrison. It stood on an expanse of uneven concrete, surrounded on three sides by a hurricane fence which had been placed there, perhaps, to catch wind-borne paper bags and candy wrappers. It was a square, symmetrical building with high windows that had to be worked by long poles. There we did elaborate multiplication and division, working on pulpy tablet paper with thick black pencils. Lucille was a grade behind me, so we were together only in study hall and at lunchtime. Then we stood apart and hugged our ribs, and looked back over our shoulders. Because we were quiet we were considered docile, and because our work was not exceptionally good or bad we were left alone. Hours of tedium were relieved by occasional minor humiliations, as, for example, when our

fingernails were checked for cleanliness. Once I was required to stand by my desk and recite "I Heard a Fly Buzz
When I Died." My cold, visceral dread of school I had
learned to ignore. It was a discomfort that was not to be
relieved, like an itch in an amputated limb. I had won the
attendance prize for my grade in the last year of my
grandmother's life, and it might never have occurred to me
not to go to school if it had not occurred to Lucille. But one
morning she was accused of looking over someone's shoulder during a history test. The next day was Saturday, but the
following week she stayed home with a series of symptoms
which did not worry Sylvie because they never included
fever or loss of appetite. After an absence of more than three
days, the school required a note from a doctor. But Lucille
had not wanted to see the doctor, and had never really
seemed ill enough to need to, as Sylvie explained in a note
to the principal. "Look at this," Lucille said. We were
walking to school together, Lucille with Sylvie's note. It was
a piece of flowered stationery folded over twice. On it Sylvie
had written, in her loopy, liquid hand, "Please excuse
Lucille's absence. She had pains in her wrists and knees, a
buzzing in her ears, a sore tongue, faintness, a stomach-
ache, and double vision, but no fever or loss of appetite. I
did not call the doctor, because she always seemed quite
well by 9:30 or 10:00 in the morning."

"We'll have to get her to write another note," I said. "Say
you lost that one." Lucille crushed the note into a little ball
and dropped it behind a tree.

"What if they call her?"

"She never answers the phone."

"Well, they might send someone to get her."

"I don't think they will."

"What if they do?"

The prospect was painful. Sylvie knew nothing about the
history test, and we would have no chance to explain it to
her. Lucille was much too indifferent to school ever to be

guilty of cheating, and it was only an evil fate that had prompted her to write Simon Bolivar, and the girl in front of her to write Simon Bolivar, when the answer was obviously General Santa Anna. This was the only error either of them made, and so their papers were identical. Lucille was astonished to find that the teacher was so easily convinced of her guilt, so immovably persuaded of it, calling her up in front of the class and demanding that she account for the identical papers. Lucille writhed under this violation of her anonymity. At the mere thought of school, her ears turned red. And now, possibly, Sylvie would be brought to school and the whole matter gone into again, and Lucille accused again, this time not only of cheating but of lying and truancy.

"I'm not going to school," she said.

"What are you going to tell Sylvie?"

"Maybe I won't go home."

"Where will you go?"

"Down to the lake."

"It will be cold."

Lucille shrugged.

"I'll go, too," I said.

Lucille said, "Then we'll both be in trouble."

The prospect seemed oddly familiar and comfortable. We walked back to the railroad and followed the tracks down to the lake. We expected someone to step out from behind a rabbit hutch or a tree or the sheets on a clothesline and question us, but no one did.

We spent the whole of that week at the lake. At first we tried to decide how to get ourselves back into school—for the difficulty was no longer just Lucille's. The problem of inventing excuses for us both baffled us, and after the third day, when, in theory, both of us would need doctor's excuses, we decided that we had no choice but to wait until we were apprehended. It seemed to us that we were cruelly banished from a place where we had no desire to be, and that we could not return there of our own will but must wait to return under duress and compulsion. Of course our aunt Sylvie knew nothing of our truancies, and so there would be her to face. All of this was too dreadful to consider, and every aspect of the situation grew worse with every day that passed, until we began to find a giddy and heavy-hearted pleasure in it. The combined effects of cold, tedium, guilt, loneliness, and dread sharpened our senses wonderfully.

The days were unnaturally lengthy and spacious. We felt small in the landscape, and out of place. We usually walked up a little sheltered beach where there had once been a dock, and there were still six pilings, upon which, typically, perched five gulls. At intervals the gull on the northernmost piling departed with four cries, and all the other gulls fluttered northward by one piling. Then the sojourner would return and alight on the southernmost piling. This sequence was repeated again and again, with only clumsy and accidental variations. We sat on the beach just above the place where the water wet it and sorted stones. (Fingerbone had at the best a rim or lip of sand three or four feet wide—its beaches were mostly edged with little pebbles half the size of peas.) Some of these stones were a mossy and vegetable green, and some were as white as bits of tooth, and some of them were hazel, and some of them looked like rock candy. Farther up the beach were tufts of grasses from the year before, and leafless vines, and sodden leaves and broken ferns, and the black, dull, musky, dormant woods. The lake was full of quiet waves, and smelled cold, and smelled of fish.

It was Thursday that we saw Sylvie at the shore. She did not see us. We were sitting on a log talking about this and that, and waiting for another cold hour to be gone, when we saw her down the beach, very near the water, with her hands in her coat pockets. "She's looking for us," Lucille said, but she only looked across the lake, or up at the sky if a gull cried, or at the sand and the water at her feet. We sat very still. Nevertheless, she should have seen us. We were almost accustomed by that time to the fact that Sylvie's thoughts were elsewhere, but having waited so many days for someone to come for us, we found her obliviousness irksome. She stood looking at the lake for a long time, her hands deep in the pockets of her big, drab coat and her head to one side, and lifted, as if she hardly felt the cold at all. We heard a train whistle across the lake, and then we saw the train creep out of the woods and onto the bridge, its plump white plume tilted and smeared a little by the wind. From such a distance it seemed a slight thing, but we all watched it, perhaps struck by the steady purpose with which it moved, as methodical as a caterpillar on a straw. After the train had crossed the bridge and sounded its whistle one last, long time, just when it would have been passing behind our house, Sylvie began to walk back toward the bridge. We followed, very slowly because Sylvie walked very slowly, and at a distance behind her. She nodded at two men in plaid jackets and dusty black pants who were sitting on their heels under the bridge, and they exchanged pleasant-sounding words we could not hear. She walked up the bank, and stood looking across the bridge for a moment, and then she began carefully, tie by tie, out onto it. Slowly she walked on and on, until she was perhaps fifty feet out over the water. Lucille and I stopped and watched our aunt, with her fisted hands pushed against the bottoms of her pockets, glancing up now and then at the water and at the sky. The wind was strong enough to press her coat against her side and legs, and to flutter her hair. The elder of the hoboes stepped out from under the bridge and looked up at her.

"Ain't our business," the younger one said. They picked up their hats and strolled off down the beach in the other direction.

Sylvie stood still and let the wind billow her coat. She seemed to become more confident of her balance after a moment. She peered cautiously over the side of the bridge where the water slapped at the pilings. Then she glanced up the shore and saw us watching her. She waved. Lucille said, "Oh." Sylvie made her way back to the shore a little hurriedly, smiling. "I had no idea it was so late!" she called as we walked toward her. "I thought it would be an hour or so until school was out."

"School isn't out," Lucille said.

"Well, I was right after all, then. The 1:35 just went through a little while ago, so it must be pretty early still." We walked with Sylvie along the railroad tracks toward home. She said, "I've always wondered what it would be like."

"What was it like?" Lucille asked. Her voice was small and flat and tensely composed.

Sylvie shrugged and laughed. "Cold. Windy."

Lucille said, "You just did it to see what it was like?"

"I suppose so."

"What if you fell in?"

"Oh," Sylvie said. "I was pretty careful."

"If you fell in, everyone would think you did it on purpose," Lucille said. "Even us."

Sylvie reflected a moment. "I suppose that's true." She glanced down at Lucille's face. "I didn't mean to upset you."

"I know," Lucille said.

"I thought you would be in school."

"We didn't go to school this week."

"But, you see, I didn't know that. It never crossed my mind that you'd be here." Sylvie's voice was gentle, and she touched Lucille's hair.

We were very upset, all the same, for reasons too numerous to mention. Clearly our aunt was not a stable person. At the time we did not put this thought into words. It existed between us as a sort of undifferentiated attentiveness to all the details of her appearance and behavior. At first this took the form of sudden awakening in the middle of the night, though how the sounds that woke us were to be interpreted we were never sure. Sometimes they occurred in our heads, or in the woods, and only seemed to be Sylvie singing, because once or twice we had awakened in the middle of the night when most assuredly we did hear Sylvie singing, though the next morning we disagreed about what the song had been. We thought we sometimes heard her leave the house, and once when we got out of bed, we found her playing solitaire in the kitchen, and once we found her sitting on the back porch steps, and once we found her standing in the orchard. Sleep itself compounded our difficulties. The furtive closing of a door is a sound the wind can make a dozen times in an hour. A flow of damp air from the lake can make any house feel empty. Such currents pull one's dreams after them, and one's own dread is always mirrored upon the dread that inheres in things. For example, when Sylvie looked over the bridge she must have seen herself in the water at the foot of the trestle. But as surely as we tried to stay awake to know for certain whether she sang, or wept, or left the house, we fell asleep and dreamed that she did.

Then there was the matter of her walking out onto the bridge. How far might she have gone had she not seen us watching her? And what if the wind had risen? And what if a train had come while she was still on the bridge? Everyone would have said that Sylvie had taken her own life, and we would not have known otherwise—as, in fact, we still did not know otherwise. For if we imagined that, while we watched, Sylvie had walked so far away that the mountains rose up and the shore was diminished, and the lake bellied and under her feet the water slid and slapped and shone, and the bridge creaked and teetered, and the sky flowed away and slid over the side of the earth, might she not have carried the experiment a step further? And then imagine that same Sylvie trudging up from the lake bottom, foundered coat and drowned sleeves and marbled lips and marble fingers and eyes flooded with the deep water that gleamed down beneath the reach of light. She might very well have said, "I've always wondered what that would be like."

We spent Friday at the shore, watching the bridge. Saturday and Sunday we spent at home with Sylvie. She sat on the floor and played Monopoly with us and told us intricate and melancholy tales of people she had known slightly, and we made popcorn. Sylvie seemed surprised and shyly pleased by our attention. She laughed at Lucille for hiding her five-hundred-dollar bills under the board, and for shuffling the Community Chest cards so thoroughly that the backs broke. I spent much of several games in jail, but Sylvie prospered, and she was full of her good fortune, and she made us each a gift of three hotels.

Monday Lucille and I went back to school. No one questioned us. Apparently it had been decided that our circumstances were special, and that was a relief, although it suggested that Sylvie had already begun to draw attention to herself. We spent the day waiting to go home, and when we came home Sylvie was there, in the kitchen, with her coat off, listening to the radio. Days and weeks passed the same way, and finally we began to think of other things.

I remember Sylvie walking through the house with a scarf tied around her hair, carrying a broom. Yet this was the time that leaves began to gather in the corners. They were leaves that had been through the winter, some of them worn to a net of veins. There were scraps of paper among them, crisp and strained from their mingling in the cold brown liquors of decay and regeneration, and on these scraps there were sometimes words. One read *Powers Meet*, and another, which had been the flap of an envelope, had a penciled message in anonymous hand: *I think of you*. Perhaps Sylvie when she swept took care not to molest them. Perhaps she sensed a Delphic niceness in the scattering of these leaves and paper, here and not elsewhere, thus and not otherwise. She had to have been aware of them because every time a door was opened anywhere in the house there was a sound from all the corners of lifting and alighting. I noticed that the leaves would be lifted up by something that came before the wind, they would tack against some impalpable movement of air several seconds before the wind was heard in the trees. Thus finely did our house become attuned to the orchard and to the particularities of weather, even in the first days of Sylvie's housekeeping. Thus did she begin by littles and perhaps unawares to ready it for wasps and bats and barn swallows. Sylvie talked a great deal about housekeeping. She soaked all the tea towels for a number of weeks in a tub of water and bleach. She emptied several cupboards and left them open to air, and once she washed half the kitchen ceiling and a door. Sylvie believed in stern solvents, and most of all in air. It was for the sake of air that she opened doors and windows, though it was probably through forgetfulness that she left them open. It was for the sake of air that on one early splendid day she wrestled my grandmother's plum-colored davenport into the front yard, where it remained until it weathered pink.

Sylvie liked to eat supper in the dark. This meant that in summer we were seldom sent to bed before ten or eleven o'clock, a freedom to which we never became accustomed. We spent days on our knees in the garden, digging caves and secret passages with kitchen spoons for our dolls, mine a defrocked bride with a balding skull and Lucille's a filthy and eyeless Rose Red. Long after we knew we were too old for dolls, we played out intricate, urgent dramas of entrapment and miraculous escape. When the evenings came they were chill because the mountains cast such long shadows over the land and over the lake. There the wind would be, quenching the warmth out of the air before the light was gone, raising the hairs on our arms and necks with its smell of frost and water and deep shade.

Then we would take our dolls inside and play on the floor in the circle of chairs and couches, by the refracted, lunar light of the vacant sky, while darkness began to fill the room, to lift the ice-blue doilies from the sodden sleeves of chairs. Just when the windows went stark blue Sylvie would call us into the kitchen. Lucille and I sat across from each other and Sylvie at the end of the table. Opposite her was a window luminous and cool as aquarium glass and warped as water. We looked at the window as we ate, and we listened to the crickets and nighthawks, which were always unnaturally loud then, perhaps because they were within the bounds that light would fix around us, or perhaps because one sense is a shield for the others and we had lost our sight.

The table would be set with watermelon pickles and canned meats, apples and jelly doughnuts and shoestring potatoes, a block of pre-sliced cheese, a bottle of milk, a bottle of catsup, and raisin bread in a stack. Sylvie liked cold food, sardines aswim in oil, little fruit pies in paper envelopes. She ate with her fingers and talked to us softly about people she had known, her friends, while we swung our legs and ate buttered bread.

Sylvie knew an old woman named Edith who came to her rest crossing the mountains in a boxcar, in December. She was wearing, besides her rubbers and her hunting jacket, two dresses and seven flannel shirts, not to keep off the cold, Sylvie said, but to show herself a woman of substance. She sailed feet first and as solemn as Lincoln from Butte to Wenatchee, where she was buried at public expense. It was such a winter, Sylvie said, so cold, that the snow was as light as chaff. Any wind would blow a hill bare and send the snow drifting, as placeless as smoke. In the face of such hard weather the old woman had grown formal and acquiescent. She had crept off to the freight yard one morning in the dark, leaving no word but a pearl ring which had never before been known to leave her hand. The pearl was brown as a horse's tooth and very small. Sylvie kept the ring in a little box with her hairpins.

Edith found her boxcar and composed herself in it, while the trainmen went about the jamming and conjoining of cold metal parts. In such weather one steps on fossils. The snow is too slight to conceal the ribs and welts, the hollows and sockets of the earth, fixed in its last extreme. But in the mountains the earth is most ceremoniously buried, with all its relics, against its next rising, in hillock and tumulus. In Butte the old woman had lain on her back and laced her fingers, and her breath had stood above her. When she arrived in Wenatchee, the ghost was gone, the exorcism accomplished. Sylvie said that she and Edith had picked berries together, and that once they had both worked in a canning factory. That winter a mutual friend had had the use of a cousin's house in Butte. The old woman had sat by the stove and sucked her fingers (in summertime there would have been unexpungeable sweet stains), and talked at trying length of other days. "You never know when you might be seeing someone for the last time," Sylvie said. When she remembered that we were there and that we were children she sometimes tried to make her stories useful.

It was with a certain Alma that Sylvie had sat one Sunday on a stack of pine boards in a lumberyard outside Orofino, waiting for the sun to rise, waiting through all the alarms, the birds' sudden risings from their woods, and the dogs' barking. It was the wind, Alma said. The wind was as rank as a hunter and never the same twice. At night it retreated into the mountains where the creatures prowl and whelp, and before day it came down again, smelling of blood. "That's what frightens the birds," Sylvie assured us, because she had never seen the sun come up but the birds first rose and cried what warning they could.

A hundred yards from the railroad track was a truck stop. Its windows lit up, and they could just hear "Irene." And farther down the road was the state institution among its fallow, isolating fields, where Sylvie and Alma had a mutual friend whom they both at that moment would have wished to see, except that too often she pulled her long hair down so that it hid her face, and wept with anger.

But when the sunlight came, after the woods were no longer black or the sky cold and high and pink, then it was excellent to drowse there while the boards breathed incense. A cat found them and lay in Sylvie's lap for a while. Alma brought back hot dogs from the café. They sang "Irene" over and over, as if to themselves. "When you're traveling," Sylvie always said, "Sundays are the best days."

Sylvie had moved downstairs, into my grandmother's room. This room was off the kitchen, three steps below the level of the rest of the ground floor on that side of the house. It had glass double doors opening into the grape arbor, which was built against the house like a lean-to, and into the orchard. It was not a bright room, but in summer it was full of the smell of grass and earth and blossoms or fruit, and the sound of bees.

The room was plainly furnished. There was a wardrobe by the double doors and a chest under the window, both built by my grandfather, as could be seen from the fact that the front legs of the wardrobe and the legs on the left side of the chest were somewhat longer than the back or right legs, to compensate for the slope of the floor. Two of the bed's legs stood on wedge-shaped blocks. All three pieces were

painted creamy white, and would have been completely
unremarkable, except that my grandfather had once orna-
mented them. On the doors of the wardrobe there appeared
to have been a hunting scene, turbaned horsemen on a
mountainside. On the head of the bed he had painted a
peacock, hennish body, emerald tail. On the dresser he had
put a wreath or garland, held in the hands of two cherubs
who swam in ether, garments trailing. Each of these designs
had been thought better of and painted out, but over years
the white paint had absorbed them, floated them up just
beneath the surface. I was always reminded of pictures,
images, in places where images never were, in marble, in
the blue net of veins at my wrists, in the pearled walls of
seashells.

My grandmother had kept, in the bottom drawer of the
chest of drawers, a collection of things, memorabilia, balls
of twine, Christmas candles, and odd socks. Lucille and I
used to delve in this drawer. Its contents were so randomly
assorted, yet so neatly arranged, that we felt some large
significance might be behind the collection as a whole. We
noted that the socks, for example, all appeared unworn.
There was a shot glass with two brass buttons in it, and that
seemed proper. There was a faded wax angel that smelled of
bayberry, and a black velvet pincushion in the shape of a
heart, in a box with a San Francisco jeweler's name on it.
There was a shoebox full of old photos, each with four
patches of black, felty paper on the back. These had clearly
been taken from a photograph album, because they were
especially significant or because they were not especially
significant. None of them was of a person or a place we
knew. Many were of formally dressed gentlemen posing in
front of a rose arbor.

In this box I found page 2 of a brochure of, it seemed,
great and obvious significance. It was slick and heavy, like
a page from *National Geographic*, and it was folded in

thirds like a letter. At the top of the page was printed, *Tens of millions in Honan Province alone.* Then there was a series of photographs. One showed a barefoot boy standing in stark sunlight, squinting at the camera. Another showed a barefoot man squatting against a wall, his face hidden in the shadow of a large hat. Another showed a young woman feeding a baby from a cup. The fourth was of three old women standing in a row, shading their eyes with their hands. The fifth was of a squinting girl and a thin pig. The pig was not facing the camera. At the foot of the page was printed, in italics, *I will make you fishers of men.* This document explained my aunt Molly's departure to my whole satisfaction. Even now I always imagine her leaning from the low side of some small boat, dropping her net through the spumy billows of the upper air. Her net would sweep the turning world unremarked as a wind in the grass, and when she began to pull it in, perhaps in a pell-mell ascension of formal gentlemen and thin pigs and old women and odd socks that would astonish this lower world, she would gather the net, so easily, until the very burden itself lay all in a heap just under the surface. One last pull of measureless power and ease would spill her catch into the boat, gasping and amazed, gleaming rainbows in the rarer light.

Such a net, such a harvesting, would put an end to all anomaly. If it swept the whole floor of heaven, it must, finally, sweep the black floor of Fingerbone, too. From there, we must imagine, would arise a great army of paleolithic and neolithic frequenters of the lake—berry gatherers and hunters and strayed children from those and all subsequent eons, down to the earliest present, to the faith-healing lady in the long, white robe who rowed a quarter of a mile out and tried to walk back in again just at sunrise, to the farmer who bet five dollars one spring that the ice was still strong enough for him to gallop his horse across. Add to them the swimmers, the boaters and canoers, and in such a crowd my mother would hardly seem remarkable. There would be a general reclaiming of fallen buttons and misplaced spectacles, of neighbors and kin, till time and error and accident were undone, and the world became comprehensible and whole. Sylvie said that in fact Molly had gone to work as a bookkeeper in a missionary hospital. It was perhaps only from watching gulls fly like sparks up the face of clouds that dragged rain the length of the lake that I imagined such an enterprise might succeed. Or it was from watching gnats sail out of the grass, or from watching some discarded leaf gleaming at the top of the wind. Ascension seemed at such times a natural law. If one added to it a law of completion—that everything must finally be made comprehensible—then some general rescue of the sort I imagined my aunt to have undertaken would be inevitable. For why do our thoughts turn to some gesture of a hand, the fall of a sleeve, some corner of a room on a particular anonymous afternoon, even when we are asleep, and even when we are so old that our thoughts have abandoned other business? What are all these fragments for, if not to be knit up finally?

I was content with Sylvie, so it was a surprise to me when I realized that Lucille had begun to regard other people with the calm, horizontal look of settled purpose with which, from a slowly sinking boat, she might have regarded a not-too-distant shore. She pulled all the sequins off the toes of the blue velveteen ballet slippers Sylvie bought us for school shoes the second spring after her arrival. Though the mud in the road still stood inches high and gleamed like aspic on either side where tires passed through the ruts, I had liked the slippers well enough. The tingling seep of water through the seams was pleasant on a spring day, when even in broad sun the slightest breeze raised the hairs on our arms.

If one pried up earth with a stick on those days, one found massed shafts of ice, slender as needles and pure as spring water. This delicate infrastructure bore us up so long as we avoided roads and puddles, until the decay of winter became general. Such delicate improvisations fail. Soon enough we foundered as often as we stepped. By that time the soles of the shoes were substantially gone. Sylvie never bought things of the best quality, not because she was close with money (although, since the money was ours, she spent it timidly, even stealthily), but because only the five-and-dime catered to her taste for the fanciful. Lucille ground her teeth when Sylvie set out shopping.

So did I, because I found, as Lucille changed, advantage in conforming my attitudes to hers. She was of the common persuasion. Time that had not come yet—an anomaly in itself—had the fiercest reality for her. It was a hard wind in her face; if she had made the world, every tree would be bent, every stone weathered, every bough stripped by that steady and contrary wind. Lucille saw in everything its potential for invidious change. She wanted worsted mittens, brown oxfords, red rubber boots. Ruffles wilted, sequins fell, satin was impossible to clean. None of the little elegances that Sylvie brought home for us was to be allowed its season. Sylvie, on her side, inhabited a millennial present. To her the deteriorations of things were always a fresh surprise, a disappointment not to be dwelt on. However a day's or a week's use might have maimed the velvet bows and plastic belts, the atomizers and gilt dresser sets, the scalloped nylon gloves and angora-trimmed anklets, Sylvie always brought us treasures.

6

The summer that followed was summer indeed. In spring I had begun to sense that Lucille's loyalties were with the other world. With fall began her tense and passionate campaign to naturalize herself to it. The months that intervened were certainly the last and perhaps the first true summer of my life.

It was very long. Lucille and I stopped going to school at the end of March, as soon as the weather relented enough to make truancy possible. As a courtesy to Sylvie we put on our school clothes every morning and walked a block in the direction of school. Where the train tracks intersected the road we followed the tracks, which led to the lake and the railroad bridge. The hoboes built on the shore in the bridge's very shadows. Our grandmother, to instill caution in us, had told us that a child who came too near a train was liable to be scalded to death where she stood by a sudden blast of steam, and that hoboes made a practice of whisking children under their coats and carrying them off. So we simply looked at the hoboes, who rarely looked at us.

We in our plaid dresses and orlon sweaters and velveteen shoes and they in their suit coats with the vestigial collars turned up and the lapels closed might have been marooned survivors of some lost pleasure craft. We and they alone might have escaped the destruction of some sleek train, some flying shuttle of business or commerce. Lucille and I might have been two of a numerous family, off to visit a grandmother in Lapwai. And they might have been touring legislators or members of a dance band. Then our being there on a bitter morning in ruined and unsuitable clothes, wordlessly looking at the water, would be entirely understandable. As it was, I thought of telling them that our grandfather still lay in a train that had slid to the lake floor long before we were born. Perhaps we all awaited a resurrection. Perhaps we expected a train to leap out of the water, caboose foremost, as if in a movie run backward, and then to continue across the bridge. The passengers would arrive, sounder than they departed, accustomed to the depths, serene about their restoration to the light, disembarking at the station in Fingerbone with a calm that quieted the astonishment of friends. Say that this resurrection was general enough to include my grandmother, and Helen, my mother. Say that Helen lifted our hair from our napes with her cold hands and gave us strawberries from her purse. Say that my grandmother pecked our brows with her whiskery lips, and then all of them went down the road to our house, my grandfather youngish and high-pocketed, just outside their conversation, like a difficult memory, or a ghost. Then Lucille and I could run off to the woods, leaving them to talk of old times, and make sandwiches for lunch and show each other snapshots.

When letters were sent to Sylvie about our days and weeks out of school, Sylvie would compose little notes to the effect that the trouble lay with the discomforts of female adolescence. Some of these notes she mailed and some she did not. At the time I thought she lied very blandly about this, considering that she was, much of the time, wholly without guile. But perhaps what she told them was only what she forgot to tell us. Lucille was, often enough, a touchy, achy, tearful creature. Her clothes began to bind and pull, to irk and exasperate her. Her tiny, child-nippled breasts filled her with shame and me with alarm. Sylvie did tell me once that Lucille would mature before I did because she had red hair, and so it transpired. While she became a small woman, I became a towering child. What twinges, what aches I felt, what gathering toward fecundity, what novel and inevitable rhythms, were the work of my strenuous imagining.

We went up into the woods. Deep between two hills was an old quarry, which we were fond of pretending we had discovered. In places the stone stood in vertical shafts, six-sided or eight-sided, the height of stools or pillars. At the center of each of them was a sunburst, a few concentric circles, faint lines the color of rust. These we took to be the ruins of an ancient civilization. If we went up to the top of the quarry, we could ease ourselves a quarter of the way down its face on our toes along a diagonal cranny, till we came to a shallow cave, just deep enough for the two of us to sit in. There was a thick tuft of grass between us, always weathered, always coarse, that we stroked and plucked as if it were the pelt of an old dog. If we fell down here, who would find us? The hoboes would find us. The bears would find us. No one would find us. The robin so red brought strawberry leaves, Lucille would sing. There was an old mine at the foot of the quarry, where someone had looked for gold or silver. It was just a round black hole, an opening no bigger than a small well, so overgrown and rounded by grass that we could not tell just where the verge was. The mine (which we only looked at and threw things into) and the cave were a great and attractive terror.

The woods themselves disturbed us. We liked the little clearings, the burned-off places where wild strawberries grew. Buttercups are the materialization of the humid yellow light one finds in such places. (Buttercups in those mountains are rare and delicate, bright, lacquered, and big on short stems. People delve them up, earth and all, and bring them home like trophies. Newspapers give prizes for the earliest ones. In gardens they perish.) But the deep woods are as dark and stiff and as full of their own odors as the parlor of an old house. We would walk among those great legs, hearing the enthralled and incessant murmurings far above our heads, like children at a funeral.

We—in recollection I feel no reluctance to speak of Lucille and myself almost as a single consciousness even through the course of that summer, though often enough she was restless and morose—we always stayed in the woods until it was evening, and when it was not bitterly cold we stayed on the shore throwing rocks into the water until it was dark. Sometimes we left when we smelled the hoboes' supper—a little like fish, a little like rubber, a little like rust—but it was not the pleasures of home at suppertime that lured us back to Sylvie's house. Say rather that the cold forced me home, and that the dark allowed Lucille to pass through the tattered peripheries of Fingerbone unobserved. It is accurate to say that Lucille went to the woods with me to escape observation. I myself felt the gaze of the world as a distorting mirror that squashed her plump and stretched me narrow. I, too, thought it was just as well to walk away from a joke so rudely persisted in. But I went to the woods for the woods' own sake, while, increasingly, Lucille seemed to be enduring a banishment there.

When we did come home Sylvie would certainly be home, too, enjoying the evening, for so she described her habit of sitting in the dark. Evening was her special time of day. She gave the word three syllables, and indeed I think she liked it so well for its tendency to smooth, to soften. She seemed to dislike the disequilibrium of counterpoising a roomful of light against a worldful of darkness. Sylvie in a house was more or less like a mermaid in a ship's cabin. She preferred it sunk in the very element it was meant to exclude. We had crickets in the pantry, squirrels in the eaves, sparrows in the attic. Lucille and I stepped through the door from sheer night to sheer night.

If the weather was cold Sylvie always had a fire in the kitchen stove when we came home. She would switch on the radio and hum domestically while she heated our soup and toasted our sandwiches. It was pleasant when she scolded us for coming in late, for playing in our school clothes, for staying out in the cold without our coats on.

One evening that summer we came into the kitchen and Sylvie was sitting in the moonlight, waiting for us. The table was already set, and we could smell that bacon had already been fried. Sylvie went to the stove and began cracking eggs on the edge of the frying pan and dropping them *shoosh* into the fat. I knew what the silence meant, and so did Lucille. It meant that on an evening so calm, so iridescently blue, so full of the chink and chafe of insects and fat old dogs dragging their chains and belling in the neighbors' dooryards—in such a boundless and luminous evening, we would feel our proximity with our finer senses. As, for example, one of two, lying still in a dark room, knows when the other is awake.

We sat listening to the rasp of the knife as Sylvie buttered and stacked the toast, bumping our heels with a soft, slow rhythm against the legs of our chairs, staring through the warped and bubbled window at the brighter darkness. Then Lucille began to scratch fiercely at her arms and her knees.

"I must have got into something," she said, and she stood up and pulled the chain of the overhead light. The window went black and the cluttered kitchen leaped, so it seemed, into being, as remote from what had gone before as this world from the primal darkness. We saw that we ate from plates that came in detergent boxes, and we drank from jelly glasses. (Sylvie had put her mother's china in boxes and stacked them in the corner by the stove—in case, she said, we should ever need it.) Lucille had startled us all, flooding the room so suddenly with light, exposing heaps of pots and dishes, the two cupboard doors which had come unhinged and were propped against the boxes of china. The tables and chairs and cupboards and doors had been painted a rich white, layer on layer, year after year, but now the last layer had ripened to the yellow of turning cream. Everywhere the paint was chipped and marred. A great shadow of soot loomed up the wall and across the ceiling above the stove, and the stove pipe and the cupboard tops were thickly felted with dust. Most dispiriting, perhaps, was the curtain on Lucille's side of the table, which had been half consumed by fire once when a birthday cake had been set too close to it. Sylvie had beaten out the flames with a back issue of *Good Housekeeping*, but she had never replaced the curtain. It had been my birthday, and the cake was a surprise, as were the pink orlon cardigan with the imitation seed pearls in the yoke and the ceramic kangaroo with the air fern in its pouch. Sylvie's pleasure in this event had been intense, and perhaps the curtain reminded her of it.

In the light we were startled and uncomfortable. Lucille yanked the chain again, so hard that the little bell at the end of it struck the ceiling, and then we sat uncomfortably in an exaggerated darkness. Lucille began swinging her legs. "Where's your husband, Sylvie?"

There was a silence a little longer than a shrug. "I doubt that *he* knows where *I* am."

"How long were you married?"

Sylvie seemed a little shocked by the question. "Why, I'm married now, Lucille."

"But then where *is* he? Is he a sailor? Is he in jail?"

Sylvie laughed. "You make him sound very mysterious."

"So he isn't in jail."

"We've been out of touch for some time."

Lucille sighed noisily and swung her legs. "I don't think you've ever *had* a husband."

Sylvie replied serenely, "Think what you like, Lucille."

By that time the crickets in the pantry were singing again, the window was luminous, the battered table and the clutter that lay on it were one chill ultramarine, the clutter of ordinary life on the deck of a drowned ship. Lucille sighed again and consented to the darkness. Sylvie was relieved and so was I. "My husband," Sylvie said, as a gesture of reconciliation, "was a soldier when I met him. He fought in the Pacific. Actually he repaired motors and things. I'll find a picture. . . ."

At first Lucille imagined that our uncle had died or disappeared in the war, and that Sylvie had been deranged by grief. She forgave Sylvie everything for a while, until Sylvie, pressed repeatedly for a picture of her husband, finally produced a photograph, clipped from a magazine, of a sailor. After that Lucille forgave her nothing. She insisted on a light at suppertime. She found three place settings of china and began demanding meat and vegetables. Sylvie gave her the grocery money. For herself Sylvie stashed saltines in her pockets, which she ate as she walked in the evening, leaving Lucille and me alone in the lighted kitchen with its blind black window.

There were other things about Sylvie's housekeeping that bothered Lucille. For example, Sylvie's room was just as my grandmother had left it, but the closet and the drawers were mostly empty, since Sylvie kept her clothes and even her hairbrush and toothpowder in a cardboard box under the bed. She slept on top of the covers, with a quilt over her, which during the daytime she pushed under the bed also. Such habits (she always slept clothed, at first with her shoes on, and then, after a month or two, with her shoes under her pillow) were clearly the habits of a transient. They offended Lucille's sense of propriety. She would imagine what some of the sleek and well-tended girls at school, whom she knew only by name and whom no possible combination of circumstances could make privy to such details of our lives, would think if they saw our aunt's feet on the pillow (for she often slept head downward as a cure for insomnia). Lucille had a familiar, Rosette Browne, whom she feared and admired, and through whose eyes she continually imagined she saw. Lucille was galled and wounded by her imagined disapprobation. Once, because it was warm, Sylvie took her quilt and her pillow outside, to sleep on the lawn. Lucille's face flushed, and her eyes brimmed. "Rosette Browne's mother takes her to Spokane for ballet lessons," she told me. "Her mother sews all the costumes. Now she's taking her to Naples for baton." Sylvie suffered in such comparisons, it was true, and yet I was reassured by her sleeping on the lawn, and now and then in the car, and by her interest in all newspapers, irrespective of their dates, and by her pork-and-bean sandwiches. It seemed to me that if she could remain transient here, she would not have to leave.

Lucille hated everything that had to do with transience. Once Sylvie came home with newspapers she had collected at the train station. At dinner she told us she had had a very nice conversation with a lady who had ridden the roads from South Dakota, en route to Portland to see her cousin hanged.

Lucille put down her fork. "Why do you get involved with such trashy people? It's embarrassing!"

Sylvie shrugged. "I didn't get involved. She couldn't even come for supper."

"You asked her?"

"She was worried that she'd miss her connection. They're always prompt about hanging people." Lucille lay her head on her arms and said nothing. "She's his only relative," Sylvie explained, "except for his father, and he's the one that was strangled . . . I thought it was kind of her to come." There was a silence. "I wouldn't say 'trashy,' Lucille. *She* didn't strangle anyone."

Lucille said nothing. Sylvie had missed the point. She could not know that Rosette Browne's mother had looked up from her sewing (Lucille told me she was embroidering dish towels for Rosette's hope chest) startled and nonplused. How could people of reasonableness and solidity respond to such tales? Lucille was at this time an intermediary between Sylvie and those demure but absolute arbiters who continually sat in judgment of our lives. Lucille might say, "Sylvie doesn't know that you don't make friends with people who fly on their backs a thousand miles, twelve inches from the ground, even to see a hanging." Rosette Browne's mother might say, "Ignorance of the law is no excuse," and Rosette Browne might say, "Ignorance of the law is the crime, Mother!" Sometimes I think Lucille tried to approach our judges as an intercessor, saying perhaps, "Sylvie means no harm." Or, "Sylvie resembles our mother." Or, "Sylvie's very pretty, when she combs her hair." Or, "Sylvie's our only relative. We thought that it was kind of her to come." Even as she offered them, Lucille must have known that such arguments were extraneous. She herself regarded Sylvie with sympathy, but no mercy, and no tolerance. Once Lucille and I were on our way to the Post Office when we saw, in the fallow little park that memorialized war dead, Sylvie lying on a bench, her ankles and her arms crossed and a newspaper tented over her face. Lucille stepped into the lilacs. "What should we do?" She was white with chagrin.

"Wake her up, I guess."

"*You* wake her up. Hurry!" Lucille took off, running toward home. I went over to the bench and lifted the newspaper. Sylvie smiled. "What a pleasant surprise," she said. "And I have a surprise." She sat up, groped in her trench-coat pocket, and pulled out a Mountain Bar. "Is that still your favorite? Look at this," Sylvie said, spreading the paper in her lap. "There's an article here about a woman in Oklahoma who lost an arm in an aircraft factory, but who still manages to support six children by giving piano lessons." Sylvie's interest in this woman struck me as generous. "Where's Lucille?"

"Home."

"Well, that's fine," Sylvie said. "I'm glad to have a chance to talk to you. You're so quiet, it's hard to know what you think." Sylvie had stood up, and we began to walk toward home.

"I suppose I don't know what I think." This confession embarrassed me. It was a source of both terror and comfort to me then that I often seemed invisible—incompletely and minimally existent, in fact. It seemed to me that I made no impact on the world, and that in exchange I was privileged to watch it unawares. But my allusion to this feeling of ghostliness sounded peculiar, and sweat started all over my body, convicting me on the spot of gross corporeality.

"Well, maybe that will change," Sylvie said. We walked a while without speaking. "Maybe it won't." I dropped a step behind and watched her face. She always spoke to me in the voice of an adult dispensing wisdom. I wanted to ask her if she knew what she thought, and if so, what the experience of that sort of knowledge was like, and if not, whether she, too, felt ghostly, as I imagined she must. I waited for Sylvie to say, "You're like me." I thought she might say, "You're like your mother." I feared and suspected that Sylvie and I were of a kind, and waited for her to claim me, but she would not. "You miss too much school," she said. "Childhood doesn't last forever. You'll be sorry someday. Pretty soon you'll be as tall as I am."

Most of the way home was along First Street, a row of cottages and bungalows with swings on their porches and shady lawns. The sidewalk on First Street was heaved and buckled like a suspended bridge in a high wind. It was shadowed by lilac and crab and pine trees that grew so near the walk that we had to bend to pass under some of them. I fell farther behind Sylvie, relieved that her thoughts seemed to have moved on to other things. Her advice to me never held her attention even as long as it held mine. We turned onto Sycamore Street, where there was no sidewalk. Sylvie walked in the road, and I followed her. This was our street. The houses were set back from the road and widely spaced. Dogs trotted out growling to sniff our ankles as we passed. Sylvie had a transient's dislike of watchdogs, and tossed sticks after them. She stood still in the road to watch a long train pass. She stripped a willow switch and broke the necks of dandelions and Queen Anne's lace that bloomed near the road. When finally we came to our house we found Lucille in the kitchen, in a tumult of cleaning, with the lights on, although it was not evening yet. "Now we find you asleep on a *bench*!" she shouted, and was unmollified by Sylvie's assurances that she had not been asleep. "Probably nobody saw her," I said.

"In the middle of town? In the middle of the afternoon?"

"I mean, *recognized* her."

"But who else—Ruthie, who else would—" Lucille threw her dish towel at the cupboards. I heard Sylvie open the front door.

"She's leaving," I said.

"She always does that. She just wanders away." Lucille picked up her dish towel and threw it at the front door.

"But what if she really leaves?"

"It couldn't be worse." Clearly Rosette Browne's mother had had Lucille on the rack that afternoon. In such cases the advocate will merge with the accused. "I don't know what keeps her here. I think she'd really rather jump on a train."

We did not know where to look for her, so Lucille turned out the lights and we sat at the kitchen table, trying to name the states of the union, and then the capitals of the states, in alphabetical order. Finally we heard her quiet steps and her tentative opening of the kitchen door. "I was afraid you'd have gone to bed. I left these on the bench today. They were too nice to waste." She opened a newspaper parcel, and we smelled huckleberries. "They're all over by the station. I had an idea about pancakes." She made Bisquick batter, and stirred the berries into it while we attempted to list all the nations of the world. "Your mother and I used to make these. We used to go to that same place when we were little girls. Liberia. We were close then, like you two."

"We always forget Latvia," Lucille said.

Sylvie said, "We always forgot Liechtenstein. Or Andorra. Or San Marino."

7

For that summer Lucille was still loyal to us. And if we were her chief problem, we were her only refuge. She and I were together, always, everywhere. Sometimes she would only be quiet, sometimes she would tell me that I ought not to look at the ground when I walked (my posture was intended not so much to conceal as to acknowledge and apologize for my increasingly excessive height), and sometimes we would try to remember our mother, though more and more we disagreed and even quarreled about what she had been like. Lucille's mother was orderly, vigorous, and sensible, a widow (more than I ever knew or she could prove) who was killed in an accident. *My* mother presided over a life so strictly simple and circumscribed that it could not have made any significant demands on her attention. She tended us with a gentle indifference that made me feel she would have liked to have been even more alone—she was the abandoner, and not the one abandoned. As for her flight into the lake, Lucille declared that the car had been stuck, that Helen had accelerated too much and lost control of it. Then why had she left us at our grandmother's, with all our things? And why had she driven her car off the road to the middle of the meadow? And why had she given the boys who helped her not just her money but her purse? Lucille accused me once of trying to defend Sylvie at our mother's expense. We were both silent for some time afterward, regretting that the comparison had been made. For by now we knew, though the certainty was not especially reassuring, that Sylvie was ours. Our mother swept and dusted, kept our anklets white, and fed us vitamins. We had never heard of Fingerbone until she brought us here, knew nothing of our grandmother until we were left to wait for her on her porch. When we were supposed to be asleep Lucille and I used to watch our mother sitting on the couch, one foot tucked under her, smoking and reading *The Saturday Evening Post*. Always at last she would raise her eyes from the page and gaze into the center of the room, sometimes so intently that one of us would get up for a drink of water and to assure ourselves that there was no one in the room with her. At last we had slid from her lap like one of those magazines full of responsible opinion about discipline and balanced meals. Sylvie could never really surprise us. As we sometimes realized, we were now in Sylvie's dream with her. In all our truancies, perhaps we never came to a place where she had not been before us. So she needed no explanation for the things we could not explain.

For example, once we spent the night in the woods. It was a Saturday, so we had worn our dungarees, and had carried our fishing poles and a creel that contained cookies and sandwiches as well as jackknives and worms. But we had not planned to stay the night, so we had no blankets.

We walked miles up the shore to a small inlet where the
water was shallow and still. These waters were full of plump
little perch disturbingly avid for capture. Only children
would trifle with such creatures, and only we among
children would walk so far for fish that bit with equal avidity
within a hundred feet of the public library. But we went
there, leaving the house at dawn, joined at the road by a fat
old bitch with a naked black belly and circles of white
around her eyes. She was called Crip, because as a puppy
she had favored one leg, and now that she was an elderly
dog she favored three. She tottered after us briskly, a
companionable gleam in her better eye. I describe her at
such length because a mile or so from town she disappeared
into the woods as if following a scent and never appeared
again. She was a dog of no special consequence, and she
passed from the world unlamented. Yet something of the
somberness with which Lucille and I remembered this
outing had to do with our last glimpse of her fat haunches
and her palsied, upright tail as she clambered up the rocks
and into the dusty dark of the woods.

It became a hot day. We rolled our jeans up in wide cuffs
and unbuttoned our blouses so that we could tie them in a
knot above our waists. Sometimes we walked on a narrow
rim of sand, but more often we limped across beaches of
round gray stones the size of crab apples. When we found
flattish stones, we skipped them. When we found stones the
shape of eggs, we threw them high, with a backward spin,
and when the water received them with a gulp, we said we
had cut the devil's throat. In some places brush and grass
grew right down to the water, and then we would wade on
slippery rocks covered with strands of silt, dim and drifting
like drowned hair. I fell in, with the creel, and then we ate
our sandwiches, because they were wet already. It was not
noon, but we planned to roast perch on green sticks and to
look for huckleberries.

The shore was littered with driftwood. There were trunks with stiff tangles of roots, and logs all stripped of their bark and spindled tight like cable. In places they were heaped, one huge carcass on another, like ivory and bones in an elephant graveyard. When we found twigs, we snapped them into finger lengths and stashed them in our pockets, to be smoked as we walked.

We walked north, with the lake on our right hand. If we looked at it, the water seemed spread over half the world. The mountains, grayed and flattened by distance, looked like remnants of a broken dam, or like the broken lip of an iron pot, just at a simmer, endlessly distilling water into light.

But the lake at our feet was plain, clear water, bottomed with smooth stones or simple mud. It was quick with small life, like any pond, as modest in its transformations of the ordinary as any puddle. Only the calm persistence with which the water touched, and touched, and touched, sifting all the little stones, jet, and white, and hazel, forced us to remember that the lake was vast, and in league with the moon (for no sublunar account could be made of its shimmering, cold life).

The sky was whited by a high, even, luminous film, and the trees had an evening darkness. The shore drifted in a long, slow curve, outward to a point, beyond which three steep islands of diminishing size continued the sweep of the land toward the depths of the lake, tentatively, like an ellipsis. The point was high and stony, crested with fir trees. At its foot a narrow margin of brown sand abstracted its crude shape into one pure curve of calligraphic delicacy, sweeping, again, toward the lake. We crossed the point at its base, climbing down its farther side to the shore of the little bay where the perch bit. A quarter of a mile beyond, a massive peninsula foreshortened the horizon, flung up against it like a barricade. Only out beyond these two reaches of land could we see the shimmer of the open lake. The sheltered water between them was glossy, dark, and rank, with cattails at its verge and water lilies in its shallows, and tadpoles, and minnows, and farther out, the *plosh* now and then of a big fish leaping after flies. Set apart from the drifts and tides and lucifactions of the open water, the surface of the bay seemed almost viscous, membranous, and here things massed and accumulated, as they do in cobwebs or in the eaves and unswept corners of a house. It was a place of distinctly domestic disorder, warm and still and replete. Lucille and I sat down and tossed pebbles at dragonflies for a while. Then we fished for a while, opening the belly of each fish as we caught it from gills to tail and gutting it with our thumbnails, tossing the guts up onto the beach for raccoons. Then we made a shallow fire, and pierced a few of the perch through the gills with a green stick, and set it up like a spit between two forked sticks. This was our invariable method, though at worst the spit collapsed and the fish dropped into the fire, and at best, which was very little better, their tail fins scorched and smoldered before the gleam of consciousness had quite left their eyes. We ate them in considerable numbers. We found ripe huckleberries on bushes that grew up among the rocks behind the shore and ate them, too. These rituals of predation engrossed us until late afternoon, and then we suddenly realized that we had stayed too long. If we had hurried back then we might have got home before it was entirely dark, but the sky was increasingly beclouded and we could not be sure of the time. Both of us were frightened at the thought of making our way along the miles of difficult shore, with the black woods above us on our right hand and only the lake on our left. If the clouds brought a wind and waves, we would be driven up into the woods, and the woods at night terrified us. "Let's stay here," Lucille said. We dragged driftwood halfway out on the point. We used a

big stone in its side as one wall, we made back and side walls
of driftwood, and we left the third side open to the lake. We
pulled down fir limbs and made a roof and floor. It was a
low and slovenly structure, to all appearances random and
accidental. Twice the roof fell. We had to sit with our chins
on our knees to avoid bringing a wall down. We sat for a
while side by side, adjusting our limbs cautiously, scratch-
ing our ankles and shoulder blades with the greatest care.
Lucille crawled out and began writing her name in pebbles
on the sand in front of the door. Evening seemed to have
struck an equilibrium. The sky and the water were one
luminous gray. The woods altogether black. The two arms
of land that enclosed the bay were like floes of darkness,
pouring into the lake from mountains brimming darkness,
but stopped and turned to stone in the brilliant ether.

We crawled into our hut and fell uneasily asleep, never
forgetting that we must keep our heels against our buttocks,
always aware of the mites and flies in the sand. I woke up in
absolute darkness. I could feel the branches at my side and
the damp at my back, and Lucille asleep against me, but I
could see nothing. Remembering that Lucille had crawled
in behind me, and that she crouched between me and the
door, I scrambled out through the roof and over the wall
into darkness no less absolute. There was no moon. In fact,
there appeared to be no sky. Apart from the steady shimmering of the lake and the rush of the woods, there were
singular, isolated lake sounds, placeless and disembodied,
and very near my ears, like sounds in a dream. There were
lisps and titters, and the sounds of stealthy approach—the
sense of a disturbing intention, its enacting inexplicably
deferred. "Lucille," I said. I could hear her stand up
through the roof. "What time do you think it is?" We could
not guess. Coyotes cried, and owls, and hawks, and loons.

It was so dark that creatures came down to the water
within a few feet of us. We could not see what they were.

Lucille began to throw stones at them. "They're supposed to be able to smell us," she grumbled. For a while she sang "Mockingbird Hill," and then she sat down beside me in our ruined stronghold, never still, never accepting that all our human boundaries were overrun.

Lucille would tell this story differently. She would say I fell asleep, but I did not. I simply let the darkness in the sky become coextensive with the darkness in my skull and bowels and bones. Everything that falls upon the eye is apparition, a sheet dropped over the world's true workings. The nerves and the brain are tricked, and one is left with dreams that these specters loose their hands from ours and walk away, the curve of the back and the swing of the coat so familiar as to imply that they should be permanent fixtures of the world, when in fact nothing is more perishable. Say that my mother was as tall as a man, and that she sometimes set me on her shoulders, so that I could splash my hands in the cold leaves above our heads. Say that my grandmother sang in her throat while she sat on her bed and we laced up her big black shoes. Such details are merely accidental. Who could know but us? And since their thoughts were bent upon other ghosts than ours, other darknesses than we had seen, why must we be left, the survivors picking among flotsam, among the small, unnoticed, unvalued clutter that was all that remained when they vanished, that only catastrophe made notable? Darkness is the only solvent. While it was dark, despite Lucille's pacing and whistling, and despite what must have been dreams (since even Sylvie came to haunt me), it seemed to me that there need not be relic, remnant, margin, residue, memento, bequest, memory, thought, track, or trace, if only the darkness could be perfect and permanent.

When the light began to come (we were warned, as Sylvie said we would be, by the roar of the woods and the cries of birds, far ahead of time) Lucille began to walk toward Fingerbone. She did not speak to me, or look back. The absolute black of the sky dulled and dimmed and blanched slowly away, and finally half a dozen daubs of cloud, dull powder pink, sailed high in a pale-green sky, rust-red at the horizon. Venus shone a heatless planetary white among these parrot colors, and earth lay unregenerate so long that it seemed to me for once all these blandishments might fail. The birds of our world were black motes in that tropic.

"It doesn't seem to get any lighter," I said.

"It will," Lucille replied. We walked along the shore, more quickly than we had walked by daylight. Our backs were stiff and our ears hummed. Both of us fell repeatedly. As we were easing our way past a mass of rocks that jutted into the lake, my feet slipped on a silty face of submerged stone and I slid full-length into the water, bruising my knee and my rib and my cheek. Lucille pulled me up by the hair.

At last it became ordinary day. Our jeans clung, our cuffs dragged, our hair hung in damp snarls. Our fingernails and our lips were blue. We had lost our fishing rods and our creel, as well as our shoes. Hunger sat heavily in our bowels, like guilt. "Sylvie will kill us," Lucille said, without conviction. We climbed up the embankment to the railroad tracks, leaving a dark trail where our passing precipitated the mists that still dimmed the weeds and grasses. The railroad ties felt warm and ordinary under our feet. We could see some of the orchard trees, twisted and crotched and stooped, barren and age-stricken. We took a little path through the trees, down to the nearest door, the door that opened into my grandmother's room. Sylvie was sitting in the kitchen, on a stool, perusing a back issue of *National Geographic*.

When we came into the kitchen Sylvie stepped down from her stool, smiling, not at us, and pushed two chairs in front of the stove. She had put two folded quilts on the wood box behind the stove. She wrapped one of them around Lucille and one around me, and we sat down. She poured boiling water and then a can of condensed milk and a quantity of sugar into the coffeepot and poured us each a cup. "Brimstone tea," she said.

"Do you know where we were last night?" Lucille asked.

Sylvie laughed. "You were dining with John Jacob Astor," she said.

"John Jacob Astor," Lucille grumbled.

The quilt was warm and soft around my arms and shoulders and my ears. I fell asleep where I sat, with the cup of brimstone tea in my lap, held carefully in both hands so as not to spill. Sleep made one sensation of heat in my palms and the sugar on my tongue. I slept precariously upright, aware of my bare feet, hearing the wood in the stove crackle. More words passed between Sylvie and Lucille, but I could not make them out. It seemed to me that whatever Lucille said, Sylvie sang back to her, but that was dreaming.

So this is all death is, I thought. Sylvie and Lucille do not notice, or perhaps they do not object. Sylvie, in fact, brought the coffeepot and warmed the cup in my hands, and arranged the quilt, which had slid from my shoulder a little. I was surprised and touched by her solicitude. She knows, I thought, and I felt like laughing. Sylvie is sitting beside the stove, flipping through old magazines, waiting for my mother. I began listening for the sound of the door opening, but after a very long time my head fell sharply to one side and I could not lift it up again. Then I realized that my mouth was open. All this time the room was filling with strangers, and there was no way for me to tell Sylvie that the tea had tipped out of my hands and wet my lap. I knew that my decay, now obvious and accelerating, should somehow be concealed for decency's sake, but Sylvie would not look up from her magazine. I began to hope for oblivion, and then I rolled out of my chair.

Sylvie looked up from her magazine. "Did you have a good sleep?" she asked.

"All right," I said. I picked up the cup and brushed at the dampness of my pant legs.

"Sleep is best when you're *really* tired," she said. "You don't just sleep. You die."

I put the cup in the sink. "Where's Lucille?"

"Upstairs."

"Sleeping?"

"I don't think so."

I went up to our room, and there was Lucille, dressed in a dark cotton skirt and a white blouse, setting her hair in pin curls.

"Have you been sleeping, too?"

Lucille shrugged. Her mouth was full of pins.

"I had a strange dream," I said. Lucille took the pins out of her mouth. "Change your clothes," she said. "I'll fix your hair." There was urgency in her manner.

I put on a plaid dress, and came to her to be buttoned. "Not that," she said. I found a yellow blouse and a brown skirt. These Lucille accepted without comment. Then she began combing the tangles out of my hair. She was not gentle or deft, nor was she patient, but she was utterly determined. "Your hair is like *straw*," she said, wetting a strand once again with her comb. Another strand uncoiled itself and the pin fell. "Aah!" She slapped my neck with the comb. "Don't move!"

"I didn't."

"Well, don't! We'll get some of that setting gel at the drugstore. Do you have any money?"

"Forty-five cents."

"I have some." Her fingers at my neck were very cold.

"Aren't you going to sleep a little?" I asked.

"I already did. I had a terrible dream. Hold still."

"What about?"

"Not about anything. I was a baby, lying on my back, yelling, and then someone came and started wrapping me up in blankets. She put them all over my face, so I couldn't breathe. She was singing and holding me, and it was sort of nice, but I could tell she was trying to smother me." Lucille shuddered.

"Do you know who it was?"

"Who?"

"The woman in the dream."

"She reminded me of Sylvie, I guess."

"Didn't you see her face?"

Lucille adjusted the angle of my head and began combing water into the hair at my nape.

"It was just a dream, Ruthie."

"What color was her hair?"

"I don't remember."

"Do you want me to tell you what I dreamed?"

"No."

Lucille tied a nylon scarf over my pin curls and another one over her own. We went downstairs. Lucille took some money from the kitchen drawer where Sylvie kept it. "My, you both look *nice!*" Sylvie said as we passed, but, as I always did when attention was drawn to my appearance, I felt very tall. By the time we reached the end of the walk I had folded my arms over the empty front of my blouse.

"You just make people notice it more," Lucille said.

"Notice what?"

"Nothing."

I felt the notice of people all over me, like the pressure of a denser medium. Lucille, impatient with my sorrows, had pried the heels off my shoes to make me shorter, but it seemed to me that without them the toes turned up. At times like this I was increasingly struck by Lucille's ability to look the way one was supposed to look. She could roll her anklets and puff her bangs to excellent effect, but try as she might, she could never do as well for me. She had even developed a sauntering sort of walk that made her hips swing a little, but the easy and casual appearance she strove for was very much compromised by my ungainliness, my buzzard's hunch. We were on our way to buy setting gel and nail polish. I hated these excursions, and I would begin to think of other things in order to endure them. That particular day I began thinking about my mother. In my dream I had waited for her confidently, as I had all those years ago when she left us in the porch. Such confidence was like a sense of imminent presence, a palpable displacement, the movement in the air before the wind comes. Or so it seemed. Yet twice I had been disappointed, if that was the word. Perhaps I had been deceived. If appearance is only a trick of the nerves, and apparition is only a lesser trick of the nerves, a less perfect illusion, then this expectation, this sense of a presence unperceived, was not particularly illusory as things in this world go. The thought comforted me. By so much was my dream less false than Lucille's. And it is probably as well to be undeceived, though perhaps it is not.

"I'm *talking* to you," Lucille said.

"I didn't hear you."

"Well, why don't you keep up with me? Then we could talk."

"What about?"

"What do other people talk about?"

I had often wondered.

"Anyway," Lucille said, "you look strange following after me like that."

"I think I'll go home."

"*Don't* go home." Lucille turned to look at me. From beneath lowered brows her eyes beseeched me fiercely. "I brought money for Cokes," she said.

So we went on to the drugstore, and while we were drinking our Cokes, two older girls whom Lucille had somehow contrived to know slightly sat down beside us and began to show us patterns and cloth they had bought to sew for school. Lucille stroked the cloth and studied the patterns so intently that the older girls became patronizing and voluble, and showed us a magazine they had bought because it was full of new hairstyles, with setting instructions. Even I was impressed by the earnestness with which Lucille studied the photographs and diagrams.

"We should get this, Ruthie," she said. I went over to the magazine stand as if to browse. The magazine stand was just inside the door. Lucille came over and stood next to me. "You're going to leave," she said. This was equally statement and accusation. I could think of no reply.

"I just want to go home," I said, and pushed the door open. Lucille grabbed me by the flesh above my elbow. "Don't!" she said, pinching me smartly for emphasis. She came with me out onto the sidewalk, still grasping the flesh of my arm. "That's *Sylvie's* house now." She whispered hissingly and looked wrath. And now I felt her nails, and her glare was more pleading and urgent. "We have to *improve* ourselves!" she said. "*Starting right now!*" she said. And again I could think of no reply.

"Well, I'll talk to you about it later," I murmured, and turned away toward home, and to my amazement, Lucille followed me—a few paces behind, and only for a block or two. Then she stopped without a word and turned and walked back to the drugstore. And I was left alone, in the gentle afternoon, indifferent to my clothes and comfortable in my skin, unimproved and without the prospect of improvement. It seemed to me then that Lucille would busy herself forever, nudging, pushing, coaxing, as if she could supply the will I lacked, to pull myself into some seemly shape and slip across the wide frontiers into that other world, where it seemed to me then I could never wish to go. For it seemed to me that nothing I had lost, or might lose, could be found there, or, to put it another way, it seemed that something I had lost might be found in Sylvie's house. As I walked toward it, and the street became more and more familiar, till the dogs that slept on the porches only lifted their heads as I passed (since Sylvie was not with me), each particular tree, and its season, and its shadow, were utterly known to me, likewise the small desolations of forgotten lilies and irises, likewise the silence of the railroad tracks in the sunlight. I had seen two of the apple trees in my grandmother's orchard die where they stood. One spring there were no leaves, but they stood there as if expectantly, their limbs almost to the ground, miming their perished fruitfulness. Every winter the orchard is flooded with snow, and every spring the waters are parted, death is undone, and every Lazarus rises, except these two. They have lost their bark and blanched white, and a wind will snap their bones, but if ever a leaf does appear, it should be no great wonder. It would be a small change, as it would be, say, for the moon to begin turning on its axis. It seemed to me that what perished need not also be lost. At Sylvie's house, my grandmother's house, so much of what I remembered I could hold in my hand—like a china cup, or a windfall apple, sour and cold from its affinity with deep earth, with only a trace of the perfume of its blossoming. Sylvie, I knew, felt the life of perished things.

And yet as I approached the house I was newly aware of the changes that had overtaken it. The lawn was knee high, an oily, dank green, and the wind sent ripples across it. It had swamped the smaller bushes and the walk and the first step of the front porch and had risen to the height of the foundation. And it seemed that if the house were not to founder, it must soon begin to float.

When Lucille came home she was carrying a bag in which there was a dress pattern with four yards of cream-

and-brown-checked wool. She explained that what seemed to me to be a dress was in fact a skirt and a small jacket. The jacket, she explained, could be worn open with a blouse or with a brown or cream skirt. The skirt could be worn with a blouse or sweater. When she had finished this outfit, she would make a brown skirt and get a sweater to match it. "It will all be coordinated," she said. "It will go with my hair." She was deeply serious. "You have to help me. The instructions tell how to do it." We cleared away the clutter on the kitchen table, which was considerable. Sylvie had taken lately to keeping tin cans. She washed the labels off with soap and hot water. There were now many of these cans on the counters and the windowsill, and they would have covered the table long since if Lucille and I had not removed them now and then. We did not object to them, despite the nuisance, because they looked very bright and sound and orderly, especially since Sylvie arranged them open end down, except for the ones she used to store peach pits and the keys from sardine and coffee cans. Frankly, we had come to the point where we could hardly object to order in any form, though we hoped that her interest in cans was a temporary aberration.

We spread the big tan sheet of instructions out on the table. Lucille knelt on a chair and leaned across the table to read step 1. "We'll need a dictionary," she said, so I went to get one from the bookcase in the living room. It was old, one of my grandfather's books. We had never used it before.

"The first thing to do," Lucille said, "is spread out the cloth. Then you pin on all the pieces of the pattern, and then you cut them out. Look up *pinking shears*." I opened to *P*. At that place there were five dried pansies—one yellow, one blue-black, one mahogany, one violet, one parchment. They were flat and stiff and dry—as rigid as butterfly wings, but much more fragile. At *Q* I found a sprig of Queen Anne's lace, which was smashed flat and looked very like dill. At *R* I found a variety of roses—red roses, which had warped the page on each side a little to their shape, and pink wild roses.

"What are you doing?" Lucille asked.

"This dictionary is full of pressed flowers," I said.

"Grandpa."

"He put lady's slippers under *O*. Probably *orchids*."

"Let me see that," Lucille said. She took the book by each end of its spine and shook it. Scores of flowers and petals fell and drifted from between the pages. Lucille kept shaking until nothing more came, and then she handed the dictionary back to me. "Pinking shears," she said.

"What will we do with these flowers?"

"Put them in the stove."

"Why do that?"

"What are they good for?" This was not a real question, of course. Lucille lowered her coppery brows and peered at me boldly, as if to say, It is no crime to harden my heart against pansies that have smothered in darkness for forty years. "Why won't you help me with my dress? You just don't want to help."

"I'll get another book to put them in."

Lucille scooped up flowers and crushed them between her palms. I tried very hard to hit her with the dictionary, but she blocked it with her left elbow, and then slapped me very deftly on the left ear. I dropped the dictionary on the floor. I was furious, of course, and determined to land a blow, but somehow she fended off every one with her bony forearms, and still managed to punch me in the ribs. "All right," I said, "I *won't* help." And I walked out of the kitchen and up the stairs.

She yelled, "You were *never* going to! *Never!*" I was amazed at her passion. I sat down on my bed with a book open, so that if she came up to rage at me more I could pretend to be reading. In a minute she stamped upstairs and stood outside the closed door. "You were just *looking* for an excuse not to help, and you *found* it! Very *nice!* Thanks a *lot!*" she yelled, and went downstairs. A few minutes later she came up again and shouted, "I can do it myself, you know! You're no help, anyway. All you ever do is just stand around like some stupid zombie!"

There was a good deal of truth in all this. I considered my uselessness exculpatory, in fact, though I wanted to make some more dignified defense, especially since I owed Lucille two blows. But that would come later. "I can't hear you, Lucille," I called sweetly. "You'll have to speak louder."

"Oh, right," she said. "Very funny. Really clever," and these were the last words she spoke to me for several days. Even Sylvie noticed. "What's gotten into you girls?" she would say. Lucille would slip out of the house, and never tell me where she was going, and she smiled with a smug delight if, just to offer conversation, I asked her where she had been. I was pretty sure that she was with the older girls we had seen at the drugstore, or with someone else who would be useful to her in the same way. Once, I noticed that she was gone from the house, and I ran out to the road. There she was, two blocks away, walking toward town. The road was deep in dust as fine as atoms, and the sun was very hot. I started running to bring myself closer to her, but she looked back and saw me and she began to run, too. I decided I would tell her that Sylvie wanted something from a store, since she was going downtown anyway. That would save me from the embarrassment of appearing to chase her. But Lucille did not stop. I ran and ran, until the stitch in my side was intolerable, and then I walked, thinking I could wave to her to stop and wait if she ever looked around, but she did not.

The flying dust made a film of mud on my skin and my sweat-soaked shirt. Lucille's, too, I thought. She will not go around all covered with dirt. She will be home. I went back to wait, savoring in anticipation a meager and minor victory, but she did not come back until the evening. Then only her face and hands were clean, her forearms and her throat and shirt were filthy. So she had spent one of those days of waiting for the day to pass, reading old magazines in the toolshed, or skipping rocks at the shore, all to avoid me.

I felt that Lucille's wrath was prolonged by the fact that she spent several hours each day working on her dress. No doubt it reminded her constantly of our quarrel, and no doubt I seemed in some part to blame for every frustration she encountered. She worked in isolation in the spare bedroom, where my grandmother's sewing machine was stored. It was a small, primitive electric. It smelled like hot rubber and axle grease, and it ran with a sound like *num-num-num. Num num num num num.* Lucille had taped a sign on the door that said, in letters of unctuous neatness and clarity, DO NOT DISTURB. It was often very quiet in that room. One day I was standing in the hall, listening to the machine and thinking that the dress might be going well enough to make a few words possible, when Lucille sang out, "Don't come in, Ruthie." For many days there was no sign that the dress would ever be done, or the hostilities ended. But one day I was sitting in the kitchen eating a sandwich and reading a book when Lucille came downstairs with her dress bundled up in her arms and stuffed it into the stove. She bunched a newspaper and pushed it in, and dropped a lighted match on it. The kitchen began to smell like smoldering hair.

Lucille sat down across from me. "I didn't even bother to take the pins out," she said.

"I'm really sorry."

"Oh, it's not your fault. You wouldn't have been any help anyway."

"I'm worse at those things than you are," I agreed.

"Much," she said.

This seemed to be something less than reconciliation.

"I'm not mad any more," Lucille said.

"Neither am I," I replied.

"I know you can't help the way you are."

I thought about that. "I know that you can't help the way you are, either," I said.

Lucille looked at me evenly. "I don't have to," she said. "I'm not like that."

"Like what?"

"Like Sylvie."

You are, too. Neither am I. Both replies seemed wrong. Lucille had a point. I suppressed an impulse to slap her, though. I knew that when she was herself trying to be so mature, a slap would catch her entirely by surprise.

I said, "I think it's pretty strange to make such a fuss over a few pressed flowers."

"It wasn't the flowers, Ruthie."

That sounded rehearsed. I waited, knowing that she would go on.

"It was much more than that. We've spent too much time together. We need other friends."

Lucille peered at me. When she had made a decision or a choice, I had little to say. She knew my side of things as well as I did. She would have considered already the fact that I had never made a friend in my life. Until recently, neither had she. We had really never had any use for friends or conventional amusements. We had spent our lives watching and listening with the constant sharp attention of children lost in the dark. It seemed that we were bewilderingly lost in a landscape that, with any light at all, would be wholly familiar. What to make of sounds and shapes, and where to put our feet. So little fell upon our senses, and all of that was suspect. One evening we were walking past the door of Sylvie's room that opened into the orchard, and we saw her brushing her hair in front of the mirror. She was sitting on the seat, with the little lamp turned on. She would brush her hair all to one side, and put down the brush and look at herself. Then she would brush it straight back, and roll it and pin it at the nape, and look at herself. All this was startling in Sylvie, who seemed to give no thought to her looks at all. My mother, Helen, had hardly shown more interest in how she looked than Sylvie herself, and yet the night before she brought us to Fingerbone she had spent the evening just that way, brushing her hair before the mirror, changing and changing, and calmly appraising each change. What was to be made of this? Nothing at all. Why should two estranged sisters think the same thoughts before their mirrors? And how do we know what Helen's thoughts were? It might not have been until she was on her way to Fingerbone that she decided what she would do, though it was in Seattle that she bought the graham crackers that were to help us wait.

It was meaningless or indecipherable, a coincidence, but Lucille and I watched her a long time. Her head fell to the side so oddly and awkwardly when she reached to fasten up the hair at her neck, as my mother's had done. That was not mysterious. They were both long and narrow women like me, and nerves like theirs walk my legs and gesture my hands. Was this coincidence just another proof of the conspiracy of the senses with the world? Appearance paints itself on bright and sliding surfaces, for example, memory and dream. Sylvie's head falls to the side and we see the blades of my mother's shoulders and the round bones at the top of her spine. Helen is the woman in the mirror, the woman in the dream, the woman remembered, the woman in the water, and her nerves guide the blind fingers that touch into place all the falling strands of Sylvie's hair.

So Lucille and I noticed things that seemed familiar to us, and possibly meaningful, and sometimes we talked

about them and often we did not. But that day she leaned
across the table and said, "I can't wait till I'm old enough to
leave this place!"

"This house?"

"This town! I think I'll go to Boston."

"No, you won't."

"You'll see."

"Why Boston?"

"Because it isn't Fingerbone, that's why!"

Every morning in August Lucille in her nightgown
touched her toes by our open window, because she had read
somewhere that good health is a form of beauty. She
brushed her red hair a hundred strokes, till it crackled and
flew after the brush. She groomed her nails. This was all in
preparation for school, since Lucille was determined now to
make something of herself. And with what rigor, what hard
purpose, she threw herself down in the grass with *Ivanhoe*
and *The Light That Failed* and *Wuthering Heights* and
Little Men and *National Geographic* and anything else she
took to be improving. She would lie in the shade, propped
on her elbows, reading, and if I said, "When you're tired of
that let's go to the lake," she replied, "Go away, Ruthie."
Sometimes I brought out a book, too, and sat down in the
grass, but her concentration distracted me and I would do
something juvenile, like pelting her book with clovers and
twigs, or laughing out loud at anything I found to be slightly
amusing in my book. She would sigh and get up and walk
into the house. If I followed her she would say, "I'll lock
myself in the bathroom if I have to, Ruthie," in a voice of
patient scorn. At this same time she began to keep a diary in
a big blue loose-leaf notebook which she tied around with a
yellow ribbon so that it would seem less like an ordinary
notebook. She left it lying on the bureau, and once I read
it. I reasoned that it contained only the things that in better

times she would have told to me. But I found instead lists of exercises she had done and pages she had read. She had copied from somewhere a table grace, which had an aristocratic sound, being brief and crisp and not excessively reverent. Beneath it she had printed in large letters, PASS TO THE LEFT. REMOVE FROM THE RIGHT. If I hoped to find anything of the old Lucille, I obviously would not find it here. But the very day I looked into the diary it disappeared from the bureau. I suppose there was something particular about the way the bow had been tied, for Lucille had grown that chary of her privacy. When it disappeared I imagined that Lucille might have begun to write down her thoughts in it, and I even began to imagine what they might be. She would surely note somewhere in it that I was more the image of Sylvie with every day that passed, because she had remarked to me once or twice that it was odd to spend as much time as I did looking out of windows, and that it was odd to tie back one's hair with grocery string.

If I had been keeping a diary at that time—Lucille's diary made me think now and then how my days would appear, entered like hers in a notebook—I would have perhaps recorded the discovery of a tattered twenty-dollar bill fastened with a safety pin to the underside of Sylvie's left lapel. This did not disturb me much. It had probably always been there. Nevertheless, it was a reminder of her transient's shifts and habits which distracted my attention from Lucille. It was now obvious that Lucille would soon be gone. She was intent upon it. I watched her constantly— here was the mystery again, and this time slowed, dilated. Every day she prepared to leave—with what care!—and someday she would leave.

On the first day of school she slipped out of the house early and left without me. I could see her walking alone, far ahead of me, in her bright white oxfords and her crisp white blouse, her hair a yellowy copper in the sunlight. Well, I thought, she is alone, too. About an hour after school began, a girl brought a note to my classroom asking me to come to the principal's office. I met Lucille in the hall, and we walked down to the office without a word. The principal was named Mr. French. He made us sit down in front of his desk, and then he sat down on a corner of the desk and swung his leg and toyed with a bit of chalk. His skull was small and smooth, and his hands were the size of a boy's and very white. He would watch the chalk in his hands and look up at us from under his eyebrows. This mannerism of his was intended, I think, to suggest a temperate yet mysterious authority, though he softened this effect somewhat by wearing loud socks.

He said, "You girls missed half a year of school last year. What are we going to do about that?"

"Give us extra homework," Lucille said. "We can catch up."

"Well," he said. "You're bright girls. You'll be all right if you make the effort. What we really have to hope for here," he said, measuring his words, "is a change of attitude."

Lucille replied, "My attitude has changed."

He looked from one to the other of us, sidelong. "So you don't need to hear my little sermon, Lucille?"

"No, I don't," she said.

"And what about you, Ruth?"

"No. I mean, I guess not."

"You guess not."

My face was very hot. Mr. French was not an unkind man, but he took an inquisitor's delight in unanswerable questions. He tossed his chalk and watched me sharply.

"She knows what you're going to say," Lucille said. "I don't know if she'll work harder this year or not. She will or she won't. You can't really talk to her about practical things. They don't matter to her."

"She's growing up," Mr. French said. "Education should matter. What *does* matter to you, Ruth?"

I shrugged. Mr. French shrugged, mocking me. "That's what I mean," he said, "by problem of attitude."

"She hasn't figured out what matters to her yet. She likes trees. Maybe she'll be a botanist or something."

Mr. French eyed me doubtfully. "Are you going to be a botanist, Ruthie?"

I said, "I don't think so."

Mr. French sighed and stood up and put down his chalk. "You're going to have to learn to speak for yourself, and think for yourself, that's for sure."

Lucille looked steadily at my face. "She has her own ways," she said quietly.

That was the only time Lucille and I spent together at school. I saw her often, but she avoided me. She became one of a group of girls who ate lunch in the Home Economics room. I ate lunch wherever I could find enough space to seat myself without appearing to wish to insinuate myself into a group, or a conversation, and I read while I ate. Lunches were terrible. I could scarcely swallow. It seemed as if I were trying to eat a peanut-butter sandwich while hanging by the neck. It was a relief to go to Latin class, where I had a familiar place in a human group, alphabetically assigned. Schoolwork itself became a sort of refuge, and I became neat and scrupulous, though sometimes I would sweat with the urge to run home and see if the house was empty. When I could fix my thoughts again on a hypotenuse, I was relieved and even happy. Mr. French, after a month or two, called me to his office to tell me he was glad to hear that my attitude had in fact changed. He had a thick stack of my neat and perfect papers lying on the corner of his desk. I knew nothing then, and I know nothing now, of the mechanics of such things as attitudes, and if it pleased him to say that I had one, and that it had changed, I would not argue. But the fact was that I preferred Latin to lunch, and to daydreaming, and I was afraid to go down to the lake alone that autumn.

Sylvie was often at the lake. Sometimes she came home with fish in her pockets. She would rinse them under the tap to get the lint out of their gills and fry them with their heads on and eat them with catsup. Lucille had grown fastidious. She lived on vegetable soup and cottage cheese, which she ate by herself in the orchard or the porch or in her room. Sylvie and I sat alone at dinner, in the dark, and we were silent. Sylvie took Lucille's absence as a rebuke, or a rebuff, and was sad about it, clearly, for she had no stories at all to tell me. "It was cold today," she would murmur, her face turned to the blue window, and her eyes as wide and mild as the eyes of a blind woman. Her hands would caress each other in a slow gesture of warming. Bones, bones, I thought, in a fine sheath of flesh like Sunday gloves. Her hands were long, and her throat long and her cheeks lank. I wondered if she could be warmed and nourished. If I were to take hold of those bone hands, could I squeeze warmth into them?

"There's still some soup left," I would say.

Sylvie would shake her head, no thank you.

One night as we sat like that, Lucille left for a dance, wearing an apricot dress she had made in the sewing room at school. She pulled her school coat over her shoulders without putting her arms in the sleeves, said good night, and went out to wait for her date by the side of the road. When Lucille closed the door behind her the house seemed very empty. I sat alone, watching Sylvie, and it seemed that she would never move. "I have something pretty to show you," Sylvie said. "A place I found. It's really very pretty. There's a little valley between two hills where someone built a house and planted an orchard and even started to dig a well. A long time ago. But the valley is very narrow, and it runs north and south, so it hardly gets any sun at all. The frost stays on the ground all day long, up until July. Some of the apple trees are still alive, but they're only as high as my shoulder. If we go there now it will be all covered with frost. The frost is so thick that the grass cracks when you step on it."

"Where is it?"

"North. I found a little boat. I don't really think it belongs to anybody. One of its oarlocks is loose, but it doesn't leak very much or anything like that."

"I'd like to go."

"Tomorrow?"

"No. I have to study tomorrow."

"We could go Monday if you like. I could write you a note."

"Monday I have a test. That's why I have to study."

"Another day, then."

"Yes."

"Are you going to study now?"

"I have to write a book report."

"What on?"

"The Prince and the Pauper."

"I don't remember much about that one."

"It's pretty good."

Sylvie said, "I should read. I don't know why I stopped. I always enjoyed it."

I went up to my room and she came up behind me. She found *Ivanhoe* on the dresser and lay down on Lucille's side of the bed, holding the book above her face. When Sylvie lay down there was nothing of crouch or sprawl. Even when she slept, her body retained the formality of posture one learns when one sleeps on park benches, and as often as not she kept her shoes on.

For some time Sylvie peered up into the book with an expression of concentration and interest. Then she lowered the book a few inches and peered up at the ceiling with just the same expression. Finally she lowered the book into her lap. Even when I sat at the vanity with my back to her, I was

aware of her lying there, and I could not keep my mind on
my work. "Sylvie," I said once, but her eyes did not change.
I waited a long time for Lucille to come home, though
when she did come I hunched over my tablet and pretended
not to notice. She came up the stairs and leaned in the
doorway.

"Hi, Ruthie."

"Hi, Lucille. Was the dance nice?"

She shrugged. "It was okay."

"Tell me about it."

"I'm tired. I'll sleep downstairs." She nodded toward
Sylvie. "You should at least throw something over her," she
said, and she went downstairs.

I lifted *Ivanhoe* out of Sylvie's hands and pulled off her
shoes and spread a quilt up to her chin. Her eyes blinked
shut and then opened again.

"Are you awake, Sylvie?"

"What? Yes." She smiled.

"What have you been thinking about?"

"Old times, mostly. People you don't know. Is Lucille
home?"

"Yes. She said she'd sleep downstairs."

"Well, we can't let her do that." Sylvie got up and slipped
on her shoes and went downstairs. In a few minutes she
came back up again and said, "Lucille isn't here."

"She has to be."

"I can't find her."

Lucille, as we learned the next morning, had walked in
her dancing dress and her apricot slippers to the home of
Miss Royce, the Home Economics teacher. She had walked
around the house, rapping at every window she could
reach, until she managed to startle the lady from her tense
slumbers, and then she was invited in and the two of them
talked the night about Lucille's troubles at home. Miss
Royce was a solitary woman, too high-strung to be capable

of friendships with children. She fluttered around her students with frightened devotion. Now and then she made a small inroad into their indifference—they would laugh at some little joke, or address some casual remark to her. Once, some of the boys had locked her in the supply closet, and once, someone had made a rabbity caricature of her face and hung it up beside the athletic trophies. At such times her eyes streamed tears. But embarrassment was dull routine for her, while acceptance was vivid and remarkable and memorable. And now here was Lucille, wandering through the dark to her house. Miss Royce gave her the spare room. In effect, she adopted her, and I had no sister after that night.

It surprised me that Lucille left so abruptly. I walked up and down Sycamore Street—not looking for her, of course, but acting as if I were, since I had no other way to soothe my disquiet. It was a windy, chilly night. I knew that Lucille would not go off in the dark by herself if she did not have somewhere to go. No one could be more concerned with Lucille's well-being than she was.

When I went back into the house Sylvie was sitting in a kitchen chair with the telephone book in her lap and her hands folded on it. "We should call the sheriff," she said.

"All right."

She opened the book and smoothed it open with her hands. "Do you think we should call him?"

"I suppose."

"It's so late," she said. "Maybe we should call him in the morning."

"He'll probably wonder why we waited so long."

"That's true," Sylvie said. She closed the book and put it aside. "It's usually best not to bother them. They have that way. Suddenly everything you do seems wrong. The simplest things." She smiled and shrugged.

"She probably went to a friend's house."

"I'm sure she's all right," Sylvie said. "I really don't want to bother the sheriff. She should come back any minute. I'll wait up for her."

The next morning Miss Royce, in her church clothes, knocked at the door. She and Sylvie talked for a while on the front step. I watched them from the parlor window—little old Miss Royce in her brown box suit with the salmon-pink bow at the throat, talking tensely and earnestly to Sylvie, who shrugged or nodded and looked to the side. Finally, Sylvie came in and went upstairs and came down again carrying Lucille's schoolbooks and her diary. She set them down on the step and Miss Royce packed them one by one into a carpet bag. Sylvie came back in before Miss Royce had finished arranging them. She sat down on the couch beside me and took up a doily and plucked at it. My grandmother's doilies used to be giant and stiff and bristling, like cactus blossoms, and now they were drab as lint, and fallen. "Lucille said you could have her things," Sylvie said. "She didn't want any of her clothes. Not even her hairbrush."

"Maybe she doesn't plan to be gone long."

"Maybe she doesn't." Sylvie smiled at me. "Poor Ruthie. Well, we'll be better friends. There are some things I want to show you."

"Tomorrow."

"That's Monday."

"You can write an excuse for me."

"All right."

8

Sylvie made up a lunch that night after supper and we set the alarm clock for five and went to sleep early, with our clothes on. Nevertheless, Sylvie had to tease me awake. She pinched my cheek and pulled my ear. Then she set my feet on the floor and pulled me up by the hands. I sat down on the bed again and fell over onto the pillow, and she laughed. "Get up!"

"In a minute."

"Now! Breakfast is ready!"

I crouched on the covers, hoarding warmth and sleep, while they passed off me like a mist. "Wake up, wake up, wake up," Sylvie said. She picked up my hand, patted it, toyed with my fingers. When I was no longer warm enough or quite asleep, I sat up. "Good girl," Sylvie said. The room was dark. When Sylvie put the light on, it still seemed sullen and full of sleep. There were cries of birds, sharp and rudimentary, that stung like sparks or hail. And even in the house I could smell how raw the wind was. That sort of wind brought out a musk in the fir trees and spread the cold breath of the lake everywhere. There was nothing out there—no smell of wood smoke or oatmeal—to hint at human comfort, and when I went outside I would be miserable. It was almost November and long before dawn, and I did not want to leave my bed.

"Come, Ruthie," Sylvie said, and pulled me by both hands toward the door.

"My shoes," I said. She stopped, still holding my hands, and I stepped into them, but she did not wait for me to tie the laces.

"Come on, come on. Down the stairs, now."

"Do we have to hurry?"

"Yes. Yes. We have to hurry." She opened the trapdoor and went down the stairs ahead of me, still pulling me by one hand. In the kitchen she stopped to scoop an egg out of the frying pan and set it on a piece of bread. "There's your breakfast," she said. "You can eat it while we walk."

"I have to tie my shoes," I said to her back as she walked out to the porch. "Wait!" but the screen door slammed behind her. I tied my shoes and found my coat and pulled it on, and ran out the door after her.

The grass was blue with frost. The road was so cold it rang as I stepped on it, and the houses and trees and sky were one flat black. A bird sang with a sound like someone scraping a pot, and was silent. I had given up all sensation to the discomforts of cold and haste and hunger, and crouched far inside myself, still sleeping. Finally, Sylvie was in front of me, and I put my hands in my pockets, and tilted my head, and strode, as she did, and it was as if I were her shadow, and moved after her only because she moved and not because I willed this pace, this pocketing of the hands, this tilt of the head. Following her required neither will nor effort. I did it in my sleep.

I walked after Sylvie down the shore, all at peace, and at ease, and I thought, We are the same. She could as well be my mother. I crouched and slept in her very shape like an unborn child.

"Wait here," Sylvie said when we came to the shore. She walked down to a place where trees grew near the water. After a few minutes she came back. "The boat is not where I left it!" she said. "Well, we'll have to look for it. I'll find it. Sometimes it takes a while, but I always find it." She climbed up onto a rock that stood out from the hillside, almost to the water, and looked up and down the shore. "I'll bet it's over there." She climbed down from the rock and began walking south. "See those trees? I found it once before, in a place just like that, all covered with branches."

"Someone was trying to hide it," I suggested.

"Can you imagine? I always put it right back where I find it. I don't care if someone else uses it. You know, so long as they don't damage it."

We walked down to where a stand of birch and aspen trees sheltered a little inlet. "This would be a perfect place for it," Sylvie said, but it was not there. "Don't be discouraged," she said. "We're so early. No one could have got to it first. Wait." She walked up into the woods. Behind a fallen log, and behind a clump of fat, low-growing pines, was a heap of pine boughs with poplar branches and brown needles and leaves. Here and there an edge or a corner of tarpaulin showed. "Look at that," Sylvie said. "Someone went to a lot of trouble." She kicked away the branches until on one side the tarpaulin and the shape of the rowboat were exposed. Then she lifted the side of the boat until it fell over upright on the heap of branches. She pulled at the tarpaulin that had been spread under the boat until she found the oars. She stuck them under the seat. The boat made a thick, warm sound as we pushed it through the pine needles. It scraped dully across some big rocks, then dragged through the sand. We pushed it into the water. "Get in," Sylvie said. "Hurry!" I climbed in and sat down on a narrow, splintery plank, facing the shore. "There's a man yelling at us," I said.

"Oh, I know!" Sylvie pushed the boat out in two long strides, and then, with a hand on each gunwale, half leaped and half pulled herself into it. The boat wallowed alarmingly. "I have to sit in that seat," she said. She stood up and turned around and stooped to hold the gunwales, and I crawled under her body and out between her legs. A stone splashed the water inches from my face, and another rattled into the bottom of the boat. Sylvie swung an oar over my head, settled it into the lock, crouched, and pulled us strongly away from the shore. A stone flew past my arm. I looked back and saw a burly man in knee boots and black pants and a red plaid jacket. I could see that he was wearing one of those shapeless felt hats that fishermen there decorate with preposterous small gleams and plumes and violent hooks. His voice was full of rage. "Just ignore him," Sylvie said. She pulled again, and we were beyond reach. The man had followed us into the water until he was up to his boot tops in it. "Lady!" he bawled. "Ignore him," Sylvie said. "He always acts like that. If he thinks someone's watching him, he just carries on more."

I turned around and watched Sylvie. Her handling of the boat was strong and easy. When we were about one hundred yards from the shore she turned the boat toward the north. The man, now back on the beach, was still yelling and dancing his wrath and pitching stones after us. "It's pitiful," Sylvie said. "He's going to have a heart attack someday."

"It must be his boat," I suggested.

Sylvie shrugged. "Or he might just be some sort of lunatic," she said. "I'm certainly not going to go back and find out." She was unperturbed by our bare escape and by her drenched loafers and the soggy skirts of her coat. I found myself wondering if this was why she came home with fish in her pockets.

"Aren't you cold, Sylvie?"

"The sun's coming up," she said. The sky above Fingerbone was a floral yellow. A few spindled clouds smoldered and glowed a most unfiery pink. And then the sun flung a long shaft over the mountain, and another, like a long-legged insect bracing itself out of its chrysalis, and then it showed above the black crest, bristly and red and improbable. In an hour it would be the ordinary sun, spreading modest and impersonal light on an ordinary world, and that thought relieved me. Sylvie continued to pull, strongly and slowly.

"You wouldn't believe how many people live out here on the islands and up in the hills," Sylvie said. "I bet there are a hundred. Or more. Sometimes you'll see a little smoke in the woods. There might be a cabin there with ten children in it."

"They just hunt and fish?"

"Mostly."

"Have you ever seen any of them?"

"I think I have," Sylvie said. "Sometimes if I think I see smoke I go walking toward it, and now and then I'm sure there are children around me. I can practically hear them."

"Oh."

"That's one reason I keep crackers in my pockets."

"I see."

Sylvie rowed on through the gilded water, smiling to herself.

"I'll tell you something. You'll probably think I'm crazy. I tried to catch one once." She laughed. "Not, you know, trap it, but lure it out with marshmallows so I could see it. What would I do with another child?"

"So you did see someone?"

"I just stuck marshmallows on the twigs of one of the apple trees, almost every day for a couple of weeks. Then I sat sort of out of sight—there's still a doorstep there with lilacs growing on both sides of it. The house itself fell into the cellar hole years ago, of course. I just sat there and waited, but it never came. I was a little bit relieved," she said. "A child like that might claw or bite. But I did want to look at it."

"This was at the place we're going to now."

Sylvie smiled and nodded. "Now you're in on my secret. Maybe you'll have better luck. And at least we don't have to hurry. It was so hard to get home in time for you and Lucille."

Sylvie pulled and then pulled, and we slid heavily through the slosh and jostle of the water. Sylvie looked at the sky and said no more. I peered over the side now and then, into the murky transparencies of the upper waters, which were clouded and crude as agate. I saw gulls' feathers and the black shapes of fish. The fragmented image of jonquil sky spilled from top to top of the rounding waves as the shine spills on silk, and gulls sailed up into the very height of the sky, still stark white when they could just be seen. To the east the mountains were eclipsed. To the west they stood in balmy light. Dawn and its excesses always reminded me of heaven, a place where I have always known I would not be comfortable. They reminded me of my grandfather's paintings, which I have always taken to be his vision of heaven. And it was he who brought us here, to this bitter, moon-pulled lake, trailing us after him unborn, like the infants he had painted on the dresser drawers, whose garments swam in some ethereal current, perhaps the rim of the vortex that would drag them down out of that enameled sky, stripped and screaming. Sylvie's oars set off vortices. She swamped some leaves and spun a feather on its curl. The current that made us sidle a little toward the center of the lake was the draw of the river, and no vortex, though my grandfather's last migration had settled him on the lake floor. It seemed that Sylvie's boat slipped down the west side of every wave. We would make a circle, and never reach a shore at all, if there were a vortex, I thought, and we would be drawn down into the darker world, where other sounds would pour into our ears until we seemed to find songs in them, and the sight of water would invade our eyes, and the taste of water would invade our bowels and unstring our bones, and we would know the seasons and customs of the place as if there were no others. Imagine my grandfather reclined how many years in his Pullman berth, regarding the morning through a small blue window. He might see us and think he was dreaming again of flushed but weightless spirits in a painted sky, buoyant in an impalpable element. And when our shadow had passed he might see the daylit moon, a jawless, socketed shard, and take it for his image in the glass. Of course he was miles away, miles south, at the foot of the bridge.

At last she pulled us toward a broad point that lay out into the lake. I could see that the mountain standing behind and against the one from which the point extended had a broken side. Stone showed pink as a scar on a dog's ear. "You can see where it is from here," Sylvie said. "They built right beside those cliffs." She brought us up against the stone and we climbed out of the boat and dragged it up on the beach. I followed Sylvie inland along the side of the point.

The mountains that walled the valley were too close, the one upon the other. The rampages of glaciers in their eons of slow violence had left the landscape in a great disorder. Out from the cleft or valley the mountains made spilled a lap of spongy earth, overgrown with brush. We walked up it along the deep, pebbly bed left by the run-off and the rain, and there we came upon the place Sylvie had told me about, stunted orchard and lilacs and stone doorstep and fallen house, all white with a brine of frost. Sylvie smiled at me. "Pretty, isn't it?"

"It's pretty, but I don't know how anyone could have wanted to *live* here."

"It's really pretty in the sunlight. You'll see in a little while."

"Well, let's not wait here, though. It's too cold."

Sylvie glanced at me, a little surprised. "But you'll want to watch for the children."

"Yes. All right."

"Well, I think you better just stay in one place and be very quiet."

"Yes, but it's too cold here."

Sylvie shrugged. "It's still early." We walked back down to the shore, and found some rocks against which we could sit, out of the wind, facing the sun. Sylvie crossed her ankles and folded her arms. She appeared to fall asleep.

After a while I said, "Sylvie?"

She smiled. "Shhh."

"Where's our lunch?"

"Still in the boat. You're probably right. It would be good if they saw you eating."

I found a bag of marshmallows among the odds and ends that Sylvie had bundled into a checkered tablecloth and brought along for lunch—a black banana, a lump of salami with a knife through it, a single yellow chicken wing like an elegant, small gesture of defeat, the bottom fifth of a bag of potato chips. I ripped the cellophane and took out marshmallows to fill my pockets. Then I sat down by Sylvie and made a small fire of driftwood and skewered one through its soft belly with a stick and held it in the flame until it caught fire. I let it burn until it was as black as a lump of coal, then I pulled off the weightless husk with my fingers and ate it, and held the creamy part that still clung to the stick in the flame until it caught fire; and so the morning passed.

Sylvie stood up and stretched, and nodded at the sun, which was a small, white, wintery sun and stood askant the zenith although it was surely noon. "We can go up there now," she said. I followed her up into the valley again and found it much changed. It was as if the light had coaxed a flowering from the frost, which before seemed barren and parched as salt. The grass shone with petal colors, and water drops spilled from all the trees as innumerably as petals. "I told you it was nice," Sylvie said.

Imagine a Carthage sown with salt, and all the sowers gone, and the seeds lain however long in the earth, till there rose finally in vegetable profusion leaves and trees of rime and brine. What flowering would there be in such a garden? Light would force each salt calyx to open in prisms, and to fruit heavily with bright globes of water—peaches and grapes are little more than that, and where the world was salt there would be greater need of slaking. For need can blossom into all the compensations it requires. To crave and to have are as like as a thing and its shadow. For when does a berry break upon the tongue as sweetly as when one longs to taste it, and when is the taste refracted into so many hues and savors of ripeness and earth, and when do our senses know any thing so utterly as when we lack it? And here again is a foreshadowing—the world will be made whole. For to wish for a hand on one's hair is all but to feel it. So whatever we may lose, very craving gives it back to us again. Though we dream and hardly know it, longing, like an angel, fosters us, smooths our hair, and brings us wild strawberries.

Sylvie was gone. She had left without a word, or a sound. I thought she must be teasing, perhaps watching me from the woods. I pretended not to know I was alone. I could see why Sylvie thought children might come here. Any child who saw once how the gleaming water spilled to the tips of branches, and rounded and dropped and pocked the softening shadows of frost at the foot of each tree, would come to see it again.

If there had been snow I would have made a statue, a woman to stand along the path, among the trees. The children would have come close, to look at her. Lot's wife was salt and barren, because she was full of loss and mourning, and looked back. But here rare flowers would gleam in her hair, and on her breast, and in her hands, and there would be children all around her, to love and marvel at her for her beauty, and to laugh at her extravagant adornments, as if they had set the flowers in her hair and thrown down all the flowers at her feet, and they would forgive her, eagerly and lavishly, for turning away, though she never asked to be forgiven. Though her hands were ice and did not touch them, she would be more than mother to them, she so calm, so still, and they such wild and orphan things.

I walked out of the valley and down the little apron of earth at its entrance. The shore was empty and, after its manner, silent. Sylvie must be up at the point, I thought. I imagined her hiding the boat more securely. That would be a reasonable precaution for her to take, convinced as she was that these woods were peopled. I sat on a log and whistled and tossed stones at the toe of my shoe. I knew why Sylvie felt there were children in the woods. I felt so, too, though I did not think so. I sat on the log pelting my shoe, because I knew that if I turned however quickly to look behind me the consciousness behind me would not still be there, and would only come closer when I turned away again. Even if it spoke just at my ear, as it seemed often at the point of doing, when I turned there would be nothing there. In that way it was persistent and teasing and ungentle, the way half-wild, lonely children are. This was something Lucille and I together would ignore, and I had been avoiding the shore all that fall, because when I was by myself and obviously lonely, too, the teasing would be much more difficult to disregard. Having a sister or a friend is like sitting at night in a lighted house. Those outside can watch you if they want, but you need not see them. You simply say, "Here are the perimeters of our attention. If you prowl around under the windows till the crickets go silent, we will pull the shades. If you wish us to suffer your envious curiosity, you must permit us not to notice it." Anyone with one solid human bond is that smug, and it is the smugness as much as the comfort and safety that lonely people covet and admire. I had been, so to speak, turned out of house now long enough to have observed this in myself. Now there was neither threshold nor sill between me and these cold, solitary children who almost breathed against my cheek and almost touched my hair. I decided to go back up and wait for Sylvie by the cellar hole, where she could not help but find me.

Daylight had moved up the eastern wall of the valley and shone warmly on the ragged and precipitous stands of black old trees that grew at those altitudes. Down below there was only shadow and a wind that swept along toward the lake just at the level of my knees. The lilacs rattled. The stone step was too cold to be sat upon. It seemed at first that there was no comfort for me here at all, so I jammed my hands in my pockets, pressed my elbows to my sides, and cursed Sylvie in my heart, and that was a relief because it gave me something to think about besides the woods. With effort, I began to think of other things. If I went down into the cellar hole, out of the wind, I could build a fire and be warm. This could not be done easily since the cellar had received the ruins of the old house.

Someone had scavenged there. Most of the shingles had been stripped from the roof, and all in all, the poles and planks that remained seemed much less than the makings of a house. The ridgepole had snapped, no doubt under the weight of snow. That was probably the beginning of the catastrophe, which might then have continued over weeks or years. I had heard of a family who lived some distance to the north of the lake who had been snowed in up to the eaves and whose house began to fall. They upended the kitchen table to prop the ridgepole in the middle, but the roof had pried loose from the walls at either end, admitting the wind, and the walls sagged the window frames out of square so that all the panes broke. They had only snow to stanch all these openings. They hardly dared make the fire in the stove hot enough to warm drinking water, they said, for fear that the snow, which was all that held the house up, would sodden and shift and pull it down. There were reputed to have been seventeen in that family. They were said to have survived by stacking themselves like firewood at night under nineteen quilts and as many hooked rugs. The mother was said to have kept a stew on the stove of water and vinegar, into which she put the tongues of all their shoes, as well as the trimmings of their hair and beards and fingernails, and pine pitch and a pair of antlers and a long-handled shoehorn—and they had lived on the pot liquor, poured over snow to stretch it. But that is a part of the world where people tend to boast of discomfort and hardship, having little else worthy of mention.

The houses in the mountains of Fingerbone were generally built as this one had been, of planks nailed to a frame vertically, and strips of wood perhaps two inches wide nailed on at each seam to close the chinks. If the house began to lean, the chinking sprang loose and the pine knots popped out and as often as not the windowpanes fell and the door could only be opened with increasing effort, until finally it could not be closed. I imagine that this kind of building was a habit acquired in a milder climate. I do not know why it was persisted in, for it turned people out of house with a frequency to startle even Fingerbone. And if the way to the next shelter was impassable because of snow, the family would not be seen again until the snow melted. The woods were full of such stories. There were so many stories, in fact, that there must have been at some time a massive exodus or depopulation, for now there were very few families in the woods, even near town—too few by far to account for such an enormous tribe of ancestors—even ancestors given, as these seem to have been, to occasional wholesale obliteration.

Abandoned homesteads like this one were rare, however, so perhaps all the tales of perished settlers were at root one tale, carried off in every direction the way one cry of alarm is carried among birds through the whole of the woods and even the sky. It might have been this house that peopled all these mountains. When it broke it might have cast them invisibly into the wind, like spores, thousands from one drab husk, or millions, for there was no reason to believe that anyone ever had heard all the tales of unsheltered folk that were in these mountains, or that anyone ever would. And that is perhaps why, when they saw me alone, they would practically tug at my sleeve. You may have noticed that people in bus stations, if they know you also are alone, will glance at you sidelong, with a look that is both piercing and intimate, and if you let them sit beside you, they will tell you long lies about numerous children who are all gone now, and mothers who were beautiful and cruel, and in every case they will tell you that they were abandoned, disappointed, or betrayed—that they should not be alone, that only remarkable events, of the kind one reads in books, could have made their condition so extreme. And that is why, even if the things they say are true, they have the quick eyes and active hands and the passion for meticulous elaboration of people who know they are lying. Because, once alone, it is impossible to believe that one could ever have been otherwise. Loneliness is an absolute discovery. When one looks from inside at a lighted window, or looks from above at the lake, one sees the image of oneself in a lighted room, the image of oneself among trees and sky—the deception is obvious, but flattering all the same. When one looks from the darkness into the light, however, one sees all the difference between here and there, this and that. Perhaps all unsheltered people are angry in their hearts, and would like to break the roof, spine, and ribs, and smash the windows and flood the floor and spindle the curtains and bloat the couch.

I began pulling loose planks out of the cellar hole, the right corner at the front. They were splintery and full of snaggled nails, but I pulled them out and tossed them onto the ground behind me, for all the world as if I had some real purpose or intention. It was difficult work, but I have often noticed that it is almost intolerable to be looked at, to be watched, when one is idle. When one is idle and alone, the embarrassments of loneliness are almost endlessly compounded. So I worked till my hair was damp and my hands were galled and tender, with what must have seemed wild hope, or desperation. I began to imagine myself a rescuer. Children had been sleeping in this fallen house. Soon I would uncover the rain-stiffened hems of their nightshirts, and their small, bone feet, the toes all fallen like petals. Perhaps it was already too late to help. They had lain under the snow through far too many winters, and that was the pity. But to cease to hope would be the final betrayal.

I imagined myself in their place—it was not hard to do this, for the appearance of relative solidity in my grandmother's house was deceptive. It was an impression created by the piano, and the scrolled couch, and the bookcases full of almanacs and Kipling and Defoe. For all the appearance these things gave of substance and solidity, they might better be considered a dangerous weight on a frail structure. I could easily imagine the piano crashing to the cellar floor with a thrum of all its strings. And then, too, our house should not have had a second story, for, if it fell while we were sleeping, we would plummet disastrously through the dark, knowing no more perhaps than that our dreams were suddenly terrible and suddenly gone. A small house was better. It broke gracefully, like some ripe pod or shell. And despite the stories I made up to myself, I knew there were no children trapped in this meager ruin. They were light and spare and thoroughly used to the cold, and it was almost a joke to them to be cast out into the woods, even if their eyes were gone and their feet were broken. It is better to have nothing, for at last even our bones will fall. It is better to have nothing.

I sat down on the grass, which was stiff with the cold, and I put my hands over my face, and I let my skin tighten, and let the chills run in ripples, like breezy water, between my shoulder blades and up my neck. I let the numbing grass touch my ankles. I thought, Sylvie is nowhere, and sometime it will be dark. I thought, Let them come unhouse me of this flesh, and pry this house apart. It was no shelter now, it only kept me here alone, and I would rather be with them, if only to see them, even if they turned away from me. If I could see my mother, it would not have to be her eyes, her hair. I would not need to touch her sleeve. There was no more the stoop of her high shoulders. The lake had taken that, I knew. It was so very long since the dark had swum her hair, and there was nothing more to dream of, but often she almost slipped through any door I saw from the side of my eye, and it was she, and not changed, and not perished. She was a music I no longer heard, that rang in my mind, itself and nothing else, lost to all sense, but not perished, not perished.

Sylvie put her hand on my back. She had knelt on the grass beside me and I had not noticed. She looked into my face and said nothing at all. She opened her coat and closed it around me, bundling me awkwardly against her so that my cheekbone pillowed on her breastbone. She swayed us to some slow song she did not sing, and I stayed very still against her and hid the awkwardness and discomfort so that she would continue to hold me and sway. My grandmother used to forget that she had stuck straight pins in the bosom of her dress, and she used to hug me much too closely in her arms, and I would be as still against her as I could, because if I squirmed at all she would put me off her lap and muss my hair and turn away.

For some reason the inside of Sylvie's coat smelled of camphor. The smell was pleasant enough, like cedar pitch or incense, curative and elegiac. Her dress was of a staunch, dry-textured cotton, and over it she wore an orlon sweater. The dress was surely brown or green, the sweater pink or yellow, but I could not see. I crouched low enough so that Sylvie's coat prevented even the seep of light through my eyelids. I said, "I didn't see them. I couldn't see them."

"I know, I know," she said. That was the song she rocked me to. I know, I know, I know. She crooned, "Another time, another time."

When we got up to leave, Sylvie slipped her coat off and put it on me. She buttoned it up, bottom to top, and pulled the wide man's collar up around my ears, and then she put her arms around my shoulders and led me down to the shore with such solicitude, as if I were blind, as if I might fall. I could feel the pleasure she took in my dependency, and more than once she stooped to look into my face. Her expression was intent and absorbed. There was nothing of distance or civility in it. It was as if she were studying her own face in a mirror. I was angry that she had left me for so long, and that she did not ask pardon or explain, and that by abandoning me she had assumed the power to bestow such a richness of grace. For in fact I wore her coat like beatitude, and her arms around me were as heartening as mercy, and I would say nothing that might make her loosen her grasp or take one step away.

The boat was already in the water, bobbing about at the end of a short rope that Sylvie had weighted down with a stone. She pulled it in and turned it so that I could step over the gunwale without getting my feet wet.

It was evening. The sky glowed like a candled egg. The water was a translucent gray, and the waves were as high as they could be without breaking. I lay down on my side in the bottom of the boat, and rested my arms and my head on the splintery plank seat. Sylvie climbed in and settled herself with a foot on either side of me. She twisted around and pushed us off with an oar, and then she began to reach and pull, reach and pull, with a strength that seemed to have no effort in it. I lay like a seed in a husk. The immense water thunked and thudded beneath my head, and I felt that our survival was owed to our slightness, that we danced through ruinous currents as dry leaves do, and were not capsized because the ruin we rode upon was meant for greater things.

I toyed with the thought that we might capsize. It was the order of the world, after all, that water should pry through the seams of husks, which, pursed and tight as they might be, are only made for breaching. It was the order of the world that the shell should fall away and that I, the nub, the sleeping germ, should swell and expand. Say that water lapped over the gunwales, and I swelled and swelled until I burst Sylvie's coat. Say that the water and I bore the rowboat down to the bottom, and I, miraculously, monstrously, drank water into all my pores until the last black cranny of my brain was a trickle, a spillet. And given that it is in the nature of water to fill and force to repletion and bursting, my skull would bulge preposterously and my back would hunch against the sky and my vastness would press my cheek hard and immovably against my knee. Then, presumably, would come parturition in some form, though my first birth had hardly deserved that name, and why should I hope for more from the second? The only true birth would be a final one, which would free us from watery darkness and the thought of watery darkness, but could such a birth be imagined? What is thought, after all, what is dreaming, but swim and flow, and the images they seem to animate? The images are the worst of it. It would be terrible to stand outside in the dark and watch a woman in a lighted room studying her face in a window, and to throw a stone at her, shattering the glass, and then to watch the window knit itself up again and the bright bits of lip and throat and hair piece themselves seamlessly again into that unknown, indifferent woman. It would be terrible to see a shattered mirror heal to show a dreaming woman tucking up her hair. And here we find our great affinity with water, for like reflections on water our thoughts will suffer no changing shock, no permanent displacement. They mock us with their seeming slightness. If they were more substantial—if they had weight and took up space—they would sink or be carried away in the general flux. But they persist, outside the brisk and ruinous energies of the world. I think it must have been my mother's plan to rupture this bright surface, to sail beneath it into very blackness, but here she was, wherever my eyes fell, and behind my eyes, whole and in fragments, a thousand images of one gesture, never dispelled but rising always, inevitably, like a drowned woman.

I slept between Sylvie's feet, and under the reach of her arms, and sometimes one of us spoke, and sometimes one of us answered. There was a pool of water under the hollow of my side, and it was almost warm. "Fingerbone," Sylvie said. I sat up on my heels. My neck was stiff and my arm and hand were asleep. There was a small, sparse scattering of lights on the shore, which was still at a considerable distance. Sylvie had brought us up to the side of the bridge and was working the oars to keep the current from carrying us under it.

I knew the bridge well. It began above the shore, some thirty feet from the edge of the water. I knew the look of its rusted bolts and tarred pilings. The structure was crude, seen from close up, though from any distance its length and the vastness of the lake made it seem fragile and attenuated. Now, in the moonlight, it loomed above us and was very black, as black as charred wood. Of course, among all these pilings and girders the waves slipped and slapped and trickled, insistent, intimate, insinuating, proprietary as rodents in a dark house. Sylvie pulled us a few feet out from the bridge and then we rode in again. "Why are we staying here, Sylvie?" I asked. "Waiting for the train," she said. If I had asked why we were waiting for the train she would have said, To see it, or she would have said, Why not, or, Since we are here anyway, we might as well watch it go by. Our little boat bobbed and wobbled, and I was appalled by the sheer liquidity of the water beneath us. If I stepped over the side, where would my foot rest? Water is almost nothing, after all. It is conspicuously different from air only in its tendency to flood and founder and drown, and even that difference may be relative rather than absolute.

The morning that my grandmother did not awaken, Lucille and I had found her crouched on her side with her feet braced against a rumple of bedclothes, her arms flung up, her head flung back, her pigtail trailing across the pillows. It was as if, drowning in air, she had leaped toward ether. What glee there must have been among the few officials who lingered, what a tossing of crepe-banded hats, what a hearty clapping of gloved hands, when my grandmother burst through the spume, so very long after the clouds had closed over the disaster, so long after all hope of rescue had been forgotten. And how they must have rushed

to wrap their coats around her, and perhaps embrace her,
all of them no doubt flushed with a sense of the considerable significance of the occasion. And my grandmother
would scan the shores to see how nearly the state of grace
resembled the state of Idaho, and to search the growing
crowds for familiar faces.

Sylvie pulled the boat some distance from the bridge. "It
shouldn't be long now," she said. The moon was bright, but
it was behind her, so I could not see her face. There was so
much moonlight that it dulled the stars, and there was a
slick of light over the whole lake, as far as I could see. In the
moonlight the boat was the color of driftwood, just as it was
by day. The tarred bridge was blacker than it was by
daylight, but only a little. The light made a sort of nimbus
around Sylvie. I could see her hair, though not the color of
her hair, and her shoulders, and the outline of her arms,
and the oars, which continually troubled fragments of
achromatic and imageless light. The lights of Fingerbone
had begun to go out, but they had added nothing to the sum
of light and could subtract nothing from it.

"How much longer?" I asked.

Sylvie said, "Hmmmm?"

"How much longer?"

Sylvie did not reply. So I sat very quietly, drawing her
coat around myself. She began to hum "Irene," so I began
to hum it, too. Finally she said, "We'll hear it before we see
it. The bridge will tremble." We both sat very quietly. Then
we began to sing "Irene." Between darkness and water the
wind was as sour as a coin, and I wished utterly to be
elsewhere, and that and the moonlight made the world
seem very broad. Sylvie had no awareness of time. For her,
hours and minutes were the names of trains—we were
waiting for the 9:52. Sylvie seemed neither patient nor
impatient, just as she seemed neither comfortable nor
uncomfortable. She was merely quiet, unless she sang, and

still, unless she pulled us outward from the bridge. I hated
waiting. If I had one particular complaint, it was that my
life seemed composed entirely of expectation. I expected—
an arrival, an explanation, an apology. There had never
been one, a fact I could have accepted, were it not true that,
just when I had got used to the limits and dimensions of one
moment, I was expelled into the next and made to wonder
again if any shapes hid in its shadows. That most moments
were substantially the same did not detract at all from the
possibility that the next moment might be utterly different.
And so the ordinary demanded unblinking attention. Any
tedious hour might be the last of its kind.

"Sylvie," I said.

She did not answer.

And any present moment was only thinking, and
thoughts bear the same relation, in mass and weight, to the
darkness they rise from, as reflections do to the water they
ride upon, and in the same way they are arbitrary, or merely
given. Anyone that leans to look into a pool is the woman
in the pool, anyone who looks into our eyes is the image in
our eyes, and these things are true without argument, and
so our thoughts reflect what passes before them. But there
are difficulties. For one, the wreck of my grandfather's train
is more vivid in my mind than it would have been if I had
seen it (for the mind's eye is not utterly baffled by darkness),
and for another, the faceless shape in front of me could as
well be Helen herself as Sylvie. I spoke to her by the name
Sylvie, and she did not answer. Then how was one to know?
And if she were Helen in my sight, how could she not be
Helen in fact?

"Sylvie!" I said.

She did not reply.

We had ridden in against the bridge again, and were
almost under it when the girders began to hum. She rested
the flat of her hand against a piling. The sound grew louder

and louder, and there was a trembling through the whole frame. The whole long bridge was as quick and tense as vertebrae, singing with one alarm, and I could not have known by the sound which direction the train would be coming from. She had rested the oars, and we bobbed farther and farther under the bridge. She folded her arms on her knees and buried her face, and she swayed and swayed and swayed, so that the boat tipped a little.

"Helen," I whispered, but she did not reply.

Then the bridge began to rumble and shake as if it would fall. Shock banged and pounded in every joint. I saw a light pass over my head like a meteor, and then I smelled hot, foul, black oil and heard the gnash of wheels along the rails. It was a very long train.

She stood up. The boat wallowed and water spilled in over our feet. She turned to look behind her. I threw my arms around a piling to steady us. The last of the train passed over our heads and sped away. She combed her fingers through her hair and said something inaudible.

"What did you say?" I shouted.

"Nothing." She gestured at the bridge and the water with upturned hands. She stared out at the moonlit lake, smoothing back her hair, and nothing in her posture suggested that she remembered she was in a boat. If she had stepped over the side, and the skirt of her dress had billowed up around her, and she had lifted her arms and slid through the rifts of moonlight into the wintering lake, I would not have been surprised.

"Sylvie," I said.

And she said, "I probably wouldn't have seen much anyway. They put the lights out so that people can sleep. I was just woolgathering, and all of a sudden it was right there on top of us. And wasn't it loud, though."

"I wish you'd sit down."

Sylvie sat down and took the oars and pulled us away

from the bridge again. "The train must be just about under us here," she said. She leaned over and peered into the water. "Lots of people came in from the hills. It was like the Fourth of July, except that the bunting was black." Sylvie laughed. She shifted around and peered over the other side.

The wind was rising, and the boat sat rather heavily in the water, because we were over our shoes in water. I scooped some of it up in my hands and spilled it over the side. Sylvie shook her head. "There is nothing to be afraid of," she said. "Nothing to be worried about. Nothing at all." She dipped her hand into the lake and let the water fall from her fingers. "The lake must be full of people," she said. "I've heard stories all my life." After a minute she laughed. "You can bet there were a lot of people on the train nobody knew about." Her hand trifled with the water as if it were not cold. "I never thought of that as stealing," she said thoughtfully. "You just find yourself an empty place, out of everyone's way—no harm done. No one even knows you're there." She was quiet for a long time. "Everyone rode that train. It was almost new, you know. De luxe. There were chandeliers in the club car. Everyone said they had ridden on it—all my old friends. Or their mothers had, or their uncles had. It was famous." She combed and sifted the water with her fingers. "So there must have been a lot of people in the freight cars. Who knows how many. All of them sleeping."

She said, "You never know."

I noticed that my feet disappeared from the ankles into a sheet of moonlight. When Sylvie moved or gestured, the light was rumpled and shadows fell over it, but just then she was lying back against the prow, trailing her hand in the water. It occurred to me to wonder whether all this moonlight together, if it could be seen from the necessary altitude, would make an image of the moon, with shadows for the sockets and the mouth.

"Aren't you cold, Sylvie?" I asked.

"Do you want to go home?"

"All right."

Sylvie took the oars and began to pull us toward Finger-bone. "I can't sleep on a train," she said. "That's something I can't do." The wind was blowing out from the shore, and the current carried us always toward the bridge. She pulled and pulled but, for all I could see, we hardly moved. Fingerbone was extinguished and the bridge pilings were one like another, so I could not be sure. But watching Sylvie seemed very much like dreaming, because the motion was always the same, and was necessary, and arduous, and without issue, and repeated, not as one motion in a series, but as the same motion repeated because here was the mystery, if one could find it. We only seemed to be tethered to the old wreck on the lake floor. It was the wind that made us hover there. It was possible to pass out of the sight of my grandfather's empty eye, though the effort was dreadful. Sylvie rested the oars and folded her arms, and we bobbed away from the shore again.

"Let me try rowing," I said. Sylvie stood up and the boat wallowed. I crawled between her legs.

My left arm has always been stronger than my right. For every two strokes with the oars together I had to take a third with the right oar alone, until I abandoned the idea of staying beside the bridge. To follow the bridge was the quickest way home, or it would have been if any progress had been possible, but as it was I let the current carry us under the bridge and toward the south. The wind was steady and the shore was inaccessible. I rested the oars. Sylvie had folded her arms and laid her head on them. I could hear her humming. She said, "I wish I had some pancakes."

I said, "I wish I had a hamburger."

"I wish I had some beef stew."

"I wish I had a piece of pie."

"I wish I had a mink coat."

"I wish I had an electric blanket."

"Don't sleep, Ruthie. I don't want to sleep."

"Neither do I."

"We'll sing."

"All right."

"Let's think of a song."

"All right."

We were quiet, listening to the wind. "What a day," Sylvie said. She laughed. "I used to know a woman who said that all the time. What a day, what a day. She made it sound so sad."

"Where is she now?"

"Who knows?" Sylvie laughed. The moon was going into eclipse behind a mountain, and the night was turning black. Sylvie had begun to hum to herself a song I did not know, and every moment was like every other, except that sometimes we turned, and sometimes a wave slapped our side.

"We could have tied the boat to the bridge," Sylvie said. "Then we'd have stayed close to town, and we wouldn't have gotten lost."

"Why didn't you do that?"

"It doesn't matter. Do you know 'Sparrow in the Treetop'?"

"I don't feel like singing."

Sylvie patted my knee. "You go to sleep if you want to," she said. "It won't make any difference."

As it happened, as the sun rose we were near the west shore of the lake, and still within sight of the bridge. Sylvie rowed us in, and we beached the boat and climbed up to the highway and walked to the railroad. I dozed on the rocks while Sylvie watched for an eastbound train. A freight came after a long time, and it slowed so cautiously for the bridge that we clambered into a boxcar without much difficulty. It was half full of wooden crates and smelled of oil and straw. There was an old Indian woman sitting in the corner with her knees drawn up and her arms between her knees. Her skin was very dark except for an albino patch on her forehead that gave her a tuft of colorless hair and one white brow. She was wrapped in a dusty purple shawl that was fringed like a piano scarf. She sucked on the fringe and watched us.

Sylvie stood in the door, looking out over the lake. "It's pretty today," she said. Portly white clouds, bellied like cherubs, sailed across the sky, and the sky and the lake were an elegant azure. One can imagine that, at the apex of the Flood, when the globe was a ball of water, came the day of divine relenting, when Noah's wife must have opened the shutters upon a morning designed to reflect an enormous good nature. We can imagine that the Deluge rippled and glistened, and that the clouds, under an altered dispensation, were purely ornamental. True, the waters were full of people—we knew the story from our childhood. The lady at her window might have wished to be with the mothers and uncles, among the dance of bones, since this is hardly a human world, here in the fatuous light, admiring the plump clouds. Looking out at the lake one could believe that the Flood had never ended. If one is lost on the water, any hill is Ararat. And below is always the accumulated past, which vanishes but does not vanish, which perishes and remains. If we imagine that Noah's wife, when she was old, found somewhere a remnant of the Deluge, she might have walked into it till her widow's dress floated above her head and the water loosened her plaited hair. And she would have left it to her sons to tell the tedious tale of generations. She was a nameless woman, and so at home among all those who were never found and never missed, who were uncommemorated, whose deaths were not re-marked, nor their begettings.

The old woman in the corner looked at me sidelong, steadily. She stuck a long finger far into her mouth to feel a tooth. Then she said, "She's gettin' growed."

Sylvie replied, "She's a good girl."

"Like you always said." The woman winked at me.

So we sailed above the water rickety click into Fingerbone, and Sylvie and I climbed down in the freight yard.

And then we walked home. Our dishevelment was considerable. But the ruin of my clothes was entirely concealed by Sylvie's coat, which hung beyond my fingertips in the sleeves, and to within an inch of my ankles. Sylvie combed back her hair with her fingers, and then hugged her ribs and assumed an expression of injured dignity. "Don't mind if they stare," she said.

We walked through town. Sylvie fixed her gaze six inches above eye level, but in fact no one stared, though many people glanced at us, and then glanced a second time. At the drugstore we passed Lucille and her friends, though Sylvie seemed not to notice. Lucille was dressed like all the others in a sweatshirt and sneakers and rolled-up jeans, and she looked after us, her hands stuck in her hip pockets. I thought I should not draw attention to myself, knowing the importance Lucille now placed upon appearances, so I simply walked on, as if unaware that she saw me.

It was a relief when we came to Sycamore Street, though the dogs all ran off the porches with their ears laid back and barked and nipped at us with a ferocity that I had never seen. "Ignore them," Sylvie said. She picked up a stone. That seemed to excite them. People came out on their porches and shouted "Here, Jeff," and "Come on home, Brutus," but the dogs seemed not to hear. Down the whole length of the street we were encircled by frenzied mongrels who made passes at our ankles. I modeled my indifference on Sylvie's.

When we were at home finally, Sylvie made a fire and we

sat by the stove. Sylvie found graham crackers and Cheer-
ios, but we were too tired to eat, so she patted my head and
went off to her room to lie down. I was almost asleep, or I
was asleep, when Lucille came into the kitchen and sat
down in Sylvie's chair. She did not say anything. She pulled
up one foot to retie a sneaker and looked around the
kitchen, and then she said, "I wish you'd take off that coat."

"My clothes are wet."

"You should change your clothes."

I was too tired to move. She brought some wood from the
porch and dropped it into the stove.

"It doesn't matter," Lucille said. "Where have you been?"

Now, I would have told Lucille, and I meant to tell her,
as soon as I composed my thoughts. I began to say, To the
lake, and To the bridge, but I felt warmly that Lucille
deserved a better answer. I wished very much, in fact, to tell
Lucille exactly where I had been, and it was precisely my
sense of the importance of telling her this that put me to
sleep. For I dreamed and dreamed that Sylvie and I were
drifting in the dark, and did not know where we were, or
that Sylvie knew and would not tell me. I dreamed that the
bridge was a chute into the lake and that, one after another,
handsome trains slid into the water without even troubling
the surface. I dreamed that the bridge was the frame of a
charred house, and that Sylvie and I were looking for the
children who lived there, and though we heard them we
could never find them. I dreamed that Sylvie was teaching
me to walk under water. To move so slowly needed patience
and grace, but she pulled me after her in the slowest waltz,
and our clothes flew like the robes of painted angels.

It seemed Lucille was talking to me. I think she said that
I need not stay with Sylvie. I believe she mentioned my
comfort. She was pinching a crease into the loose denim at
the knee of her jeans, and her brow was contracted and her
eyes were calm, and I am sure that she spoke to me in all
sober kindness, but I could not hear a word she said.

9

In the weeks that followed the sheriff came twice. He was a tall, fat man who stood with his chin tucked in and his hands folded beneath his belly and all his weight on his heels. He was dressed in a gray suit with hugely pleated pants and a jacket that was taut as upholstery in the back and upper arm. On both occasions he stood in the front door and talked about the weather. Everything in his manner suggested the deepest embarrassment. He sucked his lip and looked only at his thumbs, or at the ceiling, and his voice was barely audible. This man regularly led the Fourth of July parade, dressed in buckskins and tooled-leather boots and mounted on a broad, faded bay. He carried an oversized flag that rested in his stirrup. He was followed by the frail old chief of the Fingerbone tribe, and his half-Irish stepdaughter, and the oldest children of her first marriage. Then came the majorettes. Of course I knew

that his function was more than ceremonial. The people of
Fingerbone and its environs were very much given to
murder. And it seemed that for every pitiable crime there
was an appalling accident. What with the lake and the
railroads, and what with blizzards and floods and barn fires
and forest fires and the general availability of shotguns and
bear traps and homemade liquor and dynamite, what with
the prevalence of loneliness and religion and the rages and
ecstasies they induce, and the closeness of families, violence was inevitable. There were any number of fierce old
stories, one like another, varying only in the details of
avalanche and explosion, too sad to be told to anyone
except to strangers one was fairly certain not to meet again.
For decades this same sheriff had been summoned like a
midwife to preside over the beginnings of these stories, their
births in ditches and dark places, out of the bloody loins of
circumstance. So one must imagine he was hardened. Yet
clearly he was embarrassed to knock at our door—so
inarticulate with abashment and regret that Sylvie could
pretend the reasons for his coming were obscure.

It was not the theft of the boat he came about, though
that had been reported, nor my truancy, since I was almost
old enough to leave school if I chose to. It was not that
Sylvie had kept me out on the lake all night, because no one
knew just where we had been. It was that we returned to
Fingerbone in a freight car. Sylvie was an unredeemed
transient, and she was making a transient of me.

Fingerbone was moved to solemn pity. There was not a
soul there but knew how shallow-rooted the whole town
was. It flooded yearly, and had burned once. Often enough
the lumber mill shut down, or burned down. There were
reports that things were otherwise elsewhere, and anyone,
on a melancholy evening, might feel that Fingerbone was a
meager and difficult place.

So a diaspora threatened always. And there is no living

creature, though the whims of eons had put its eyes on
boggling stalks and clamped it in a carapace, diminished it
to a pinpoint and given it a taste for mud and stuck it down
a well or hid it under a stone, but that creature will live on
if it can. So certainly Fingerbone, which despite all its
difficulties sometimes seemed pleasant and ordinary, would
value itself, too, and live on if and as it could. So every
wanderer whose presence suggested it might be as well to
drift, or it could not matter much, was met with something
that seemed at first sight a moral reaction, since morality is
a check upon the strongest temptations. And these strangers
were fed on the stoop, and sometimes warmed at the stove,
in a spirit that seemed at first sight pity or charity, since pity
and charity may be at root an attempt to propitiate the dark
powers that have not touched us yet. When one of these
lives ended within the town jurisdiction, the preacher could
be relied upon to say "This unfortunate," as if an anonymous grave were somehow deeper than a grave with a name
above it. So the transients wandered through Fingerbone
like ghosts, terrifying as ghosts are because they were not
very different from us. And so it was important to the town
to believe that I should be rescued, and that rescue was
possible. If the sheriff felt he should not come knocking at
a door behind which no murder had been done, he had
seen more than any man should see and was to be
pardoned. It was because of his tolerance of transients that
they haunted the town as they did, sleeping in abandoned
houses and in the ruins of fallen houses, and building their
shanties and lean-tos under the bridge and along the shore.
They seldom spoke in our hearing or looked at us directly,
but we stole glimpses of their faces. They were like the
people in old photographs—we did not see them through a
veil of knowledge and habit, but simply and plainly, as they
were lined or scarred, as they were startled or blank. Like
the dead, we could consider their histories complete, and

we wondered only what had brought them to transiency, to drifting, since their lives as drifters were like pacings and broodings and skirmishings among ghosts who cannot pay their way across the Styx. However long a postscript to however short a life, it was still no part of the story. We imagined that if they spoke to us they would astonish us with tales of disaster and disgrace and bitter sorrow, that would fly into the hills and stay there in the dark earth and in the cries of birds. For in the case of such pure sorrow, who can distinguish mine from thine? The sorrow is that every soul is put out of house. Fingerbone lived always among the dispossessed. In bad times the town was flooded with them, and when they walked by in the roads at night, the children of Fingerbone pulled their quilts over their heads and muttered the old supplication that if they should die sleeping, God would see to their souls, at least.

Neighbor women and church women began to bring us casseroles and coffee cakes. They brought me knitted socks and caps and comforters. They sat on the edge of the couch with their offerings in their laps and made delicate inquiries about Sylvie's can and bottle collection. One of these ladies introduced her friend as the wife of the probate judge.

I was actually glad that Lucille was spared these scenes. First of all, neither Sylvie nor I had any thought at all of inviting neighbors in. The parlor was full of the newspapers and magazines Sylvie brought home. They were stacked pretty neatly, considering that some of them had been rolled, perhaps to swat flies. Nevertheless, they took up the end of the room where the fireplace had been. Then there were the cans stacked along the wall opposite the couch. Like the newspapers, they were stacked to the ceiling. Nevertheless, they took up considerable floor space. Of course, we could have made other arrangements, if we had planned to entertain, but we did not. The visitors glanced at

the cans and papers as if they thought Sylvie must consider
such things appropriate to a parlor. That was ridiculous. We
had simply ceased to consider that room a parlor, since,
until we had attracted the attention of these ladies, no one
ever came to call. Who would think of dusting or sweeping
the cobwebs down in a room used for the storage of cans
and newspapers—things utterly without value? Sylvie only
kept them, I think, because she considered accumulation to
be the essence of housekeeping, and because she considered
the hoarding of worthless things to be proof of a particularly
scrupulous thrift.

The kitchen was stacked with cans, and with brown paper
bags. Sylvie knew that such collecting invited mice, so she
brought home a yellow cat with half an ear and a bulging
belly, and it littered twice. The first litter was old enough
already to prey on the swallows that had begun to nest on
the second floor. That was good and useful, but the cats
often brought the birds into the parlor, and left wings and
feet and heads lying about, even on the couch.

Of course the ladies who came to our house had killed
and scalded and plucked and gutted and dismembered and
fried and eaten fowl beyond reckoning. Still, they were
startled by these remnants of swallows and sparrows, as
much as by the cats themselves, which numbered thirteen
or fourteen. So long as the ladies were seated in that room,
or in that house, I knew that their attention would never
wander, the subject would never change. I always excused
myself and went upstairs to my room and took off my shoes
and crept back down again, and by this simple ruse I
became privy to the workings of fate, my fate, at least.

In their conversations with Sylvie, there were many
silences. Sylvie would say, "It looks like winter is early this
year," and one would say, "I'll send my husband over to fix
those broken windows," and another would say, "My little
Milton'll split some kindling for you. He needs the exer-
cise." Then there would be a silence.

Sylvie would say, "Could I get you some coffee?" and one of them would say, "Don't bother, dear," and another, "We just came by to leave the mittens and the cake and the casserole," and another, "We don't want to disturb you, dear." Then there would be a silence.

One of the ladies asked Sylvie if she was not lonely in Fingerbone, or if she had found a few friends her own age. Sylvie said yes, she was lonely, and yes, it was difficult to find friends, but she was used to being lonely and did not mind it.

"But you and Ruthie are together a lot."

"Oh, all the time now. She's like another sister to me. She's her mother all over again."

There was a long silence.

The ladies who came to speak to Sylvie had a clear intention, a settled purpose, yet they were timid about threading the labyrinths of our privacy. They had some general notions of tact but very little practice in the use of it, and so they tended to err on the side of caution, to deal in indirection, and to succumb to embarrassment. They had salved the injured and tended the ill and soothed and grieved with those who mourned, obedient to Biblical injunction, and those who were too sad and solitary to want their sympathy they had fed or clothed, to the extent of their slender means, in the silence of heart that made their charity acceptable. If their good works supplied the lack of other diversions, they were good women all the same. They had been made to enact the gestures and attitudes of Christian benevolence from young girlhood, until these gestures and attitudes became habit, and the habit became so strongly engrained as to seem to be impulse or instinct. For if Fingerbone was remarkable for anything besides loneliness and murder, it was for religious zeal of the purest and rarest kind. There were, in fact, several churches whose visions of sin and salvation were so ecstatic, and so nearly identical, that the superiority of one church over another could be argued only in terms of good works. And the obligation to perform these works rested squarely with the women, since salvation was universally considered to be much more becoming in women than in men.

Their motives in coming were complex and unsearchable, but all of one general kind. They were obliged to come by their notions of piety and good breeding, and by a desire, a determination, to keep me, so to speak, safely within doors. For surely they had in recent months remarked in me a tendency to comb my hair almost never, and to twist it and chew at it continually. They had no way of knowing that I spoke at all these past few months, since I spoke only to Sylvie. So they had reason to feel that my social graces were eroding away, and that soon I would feel ill at ease in a cleanly house with glass in its windows—I would be lost to ordinary society. I would be a ghost, and their food would not answer to my hunger, and my hands could pass through their down quilts and tatted pillow covers and never feel them or find comfort in them. Like a soul released, I would find here only the images and simulacra of the things needed to sustain me. If the mountain that stood up behind Fingerbone were Vesuvius, and if one night it drowned the place in stone, and the few survivors and the curious came to view the flood and assess the damage, and to clean the mess away with dynamite and picks, they would find petrified pies and the fossils of casseroles, and be mocked by appearances. In much the same way, the tramps, when they doffed their hats and stepped into the kitchen as they might do when the weather was severe, looked into the parlor and murmured, "Nice place you have here," and the lady who stood at the elbow of any one of them knew that if she renounced her husband and cursed her children and offered all that had been theirs

to this lonely, houseless, placeless man, soon or late he
would say "Thanks" and be gone into the evening, being the
hungriest of human creatures and finding nothing here to
sustain him, leaving it all, like something dropped in a
corner by the wind. Why should they all feel judgment in
the fact that these nameless souls looked into their lighted
windows without envy and took the best of suppers as no
more than their meager due?

Imagine that Noah knocked his house apart and used the
planks to build an ark, while his neighbors looked on, full
of doubt. A house, he must have told them, should be
daubed with pitch and built to float cloud high, if need be.
A lettuce patch was of no use at all, and a good foundation
was worse than useless. A house should have a compass and
a keel. The neighbors would have put their hands in their
pockets and chewed their lips and strolled home to houses
they now found wanting in ways they could not understand.
Perhaps, pious as they were, these ladies did not wish to see
me pass into that sad and outcast state of revelation where
one begins to feel superior to one's neighbors.

"Do you hear anything from their father?"

Sylvie must have shaken her head.

"Or Mr. Fisher?"

"Who?"

"Your husband, dear."

Sylvie laughed.

There was a long silence.

Finally someone said, "Do you know why we're asking all
these questions?"

Maybe Sylvie nodded, or shook her head. She said
nothing.

The lady persisted. "Some people—some of us—feel that
Ruthie should have—that a young girl needs an orderly
life."

"She's had so much trouble and sorrow." So much, yes,
she has, it's the Lord's truth, it's a pity. It is.

"Really, she's all right," Sylvie answered.

Murmurs. One of them said, "She looks so sad."

And Sylvie replied, "Well, she *is* sad."

Silence.

Sylvie said, "She should be sad." She laughed. "I don't mean she *should* be, but, you know, who wouldn't be?"

Again, silence.

"That's how it is with family," Sylvie said. "You feel them the most when they're gone. I knew a woman once who had four children, and she didn't seem to care for them at all. She'd give them string beans for breakfast, and she never even cared if their shoes matched. That's what people told me. But I knew her when she was old, and she had nine little beds in her house, all made up, and every night she'd go from one to another, tucking the children in, over and over again. She just had four, but after they were all gone she had nine! Well, she was probably crazy. But you know what I mean. Helen and Papa were never close."

Silence.

"Now I look at Ruthie and I see Helen, too. That's why families are so important. Other people walk out the door and they're gone!"

Silence. A shifting of the couch.

"Families should stay together. Otherwise things get out of control. My father, you know. I can't even remember what he was like, I mean when he was alive. But ever since, it's Papa here and Papa there, and dreams . . . Like the poor woman with nine children. She was walking the floor the whole night!"

No one said anything for a long time. Finally someone said, "Families are a sorrow, and that's the truth," and another one said, "I lost my girl sixteen years ago in June and her face is before me now," and someone else said, "If you can keep them, that's bad enough, but if you lose them—" The world is full of trouble. Yes it is.

"Families should stay together," Sylvie said. "They should. There is no other help. Ruthie and I have trouble enough with the ones we've lost already." The ladies seemed absorbed in thoughts of their own. Finally someone said, "But, Sylvie, you have to keep her off the freight trains."

"What?"

"She shouldn't be riding around in freight cars."

"Oh, no." Sylvie laughed. "That was just the one time. We were so tired, you know. We'd been out all night, and we just took the fastest way home."

"Out where?"

"On the lake."

Murmurs. "In that little boat?"

"It's a perfectly good boat. It doesn't look like much but it's all right."

The ladies said goodbye, and left their offerings on the couch.

I came in and sat on the floor with Sylvie, and we ate bits and morsels from the pots and plates they had left behind.

"Did you hear what they said?" Sylvie asked.

"Mm-hmm."

"What did you think?"

The room was dark. The cans in their towering stack gleamed blue and the effect was cold and melancholy. I said, "I don't want to talk."

"I don't know what to think," Sylvie said. "We could fix it up around here," she said finally. "Some of this stuff could go out to the shed, I suppose."

The next day I combed my hair and went to school, and when I came home Sylvie had emptied the parlor of cans entirely and had begun to remove the newspapers. She had put a bouquet of artificial flowers on the kitchen table, and she was frying chicken. "Now, isn't this nice?" she asked, and then, "Did you have a nice day at school?"

Sylvie was pretty, but she was prettiest when something had just startled her into feeling that the world had to be dealt with in some way, and then she undertook the most ordinary things with an arch, tense, tentative good will that made them seem difficult and remarkable, and she was delighted by even partial successes.

"School was fine," I said. It was terrible. I had outgrown my dress, and whenever I ceased to control myself by a conscious effort of will, my feet began to dance or I bit my knuckles or twisted my hair. I could not appear to pay attention to the teacher for fear she might call on me and I would suddenly be the center of attention. I drew elaborate shapes all over my tablet, which I changed whenever they seemed on the point of becoming recognizable. This was to divert my thoughts from the impulse to walk out of the room, which was very strong, although I could count on the benignity of Miss Knoll, who was so obese that she wore laceless sneakers and the tongues popped up, and who wept when she read Keats and was ashamed.

"Did you see Lucille?"

"No." Yes. Lucille was everywhere, but we did not speak.

"Maybe she's sick. Maybe I should go over there and find out how she is. I'm her aunt."

"Yes." What could it matter? It seemed to me that the fragility of our household was by now so great that the breach was inevitable, and so it was futile to worry whether there was wisdom or sense in any particular scheme to save it. One thing or another would put an end to it soon.

"I'll take her some chicken," Sylvie said. Yes, take her some chicken. Sylvie was so struck with this idea that she set apart the neck for herself and the wings for me and bundled all the rest into a tea towel. She washed her hands and pinned back her hair and set off for Lucille's.

It was late when she came back. I had chewed at the chicken wings and gone to bed with *Not as a Stranger*. She came upstairs and sat down at the foot of the bed. "Those women have been talking to Lucille," she said. "Do you know what they want to do?"

"Yes."

"Lucille told me. I don't think they can do it, do you?"

"No." Yes.

"I don't think so, either. It would be terrible. They know that."

"Yes." Yes. It would be terrible. They know that.

"I thought they just wanted to talk about the freight train. I thought they understood. But Lucille says now it's because we spent the night on the lake. Well, I'll explain to them."

Explain to them, Sylvie.

"Don't worry." She patted the lump my knee made in the blanket. "I'll explain it all to them." I finally fell asleep despite the noise Sylvie made washing and stacking dishes. In the morning the kitchen table was cleared and scrubbed and there was a bowl and a spoon and a box of cornflakes and a glass of orange juice and two pieces of buttered toast on a saucer and the vase of artificial daisies. Sylvie was filthy with newsprint and there were cobwebs in her hair.

"This is nice," I said.

She nodded. "What a mess! Honestly. I was up the whole night. Now, you eat breakfast. You'll be late for school."

"Do you think I should stay home and help?"

"No! You go to school, Ruthie. I'll help you brush out your hair. You've got to look nice."

I had never imagined that Sylvie was capable of haste or urgency. I was surprised, in fact, that she would go to such lengths for my sake. It had always seemed to me that Sylvie and I were there together purely as a matter of accident— the wind blows a milkweed puff and two seeds do not fly. It seemed to me that we shared the house amicably because it was spacious enough and we both felt at home there and because habits of politeness were deeply engrained in us

both. If a judge were to appear and whisk me under his
black robes like a hobo in our grandmother's cautionary
tales, and carry me off to the rumored farm, a shock would
roll through the house, and rattle the plates, and totter the
cups, and ring in the glasses for days, perhaps, and Sylvie
would have another story to tell, not so very sad compared
with others. Yet here was purpose and urgency. I knew we
were doomed. I put on a skirt which Sylvie had let down for
me and pressed (things like that matter to them, she said),
and my best sweater, and Sylvie worried the largest snarls
out of my hair with a wide-tooth comb. "Now stand up
straight," she said as I went out the door. "Smile at people."
I spent the day in misery and suspense, and I came home to
find Sylvie sitting in a swept and catless parlor, speaking
softly with the sheriff.

  It is a terrible thing to break up a family. If you
understand that, you will understand everything that fol-
lows. The sheriff knew it as well as anyone, and his face was
slack with regret. "There'll be a hearing, Mrs. Fisher," he
said, wearily, because whatever Sylvie might say, he could
make no other reply.

  "It would be a terrible thing to do," Sylvie said, and the
sheriff dropped his palms on his knees by way of agreement
and said, "There'll be a hearing, ma'am." When I came
into the room he rose and clutched his hat under his belly.
He had all the formality of manner of an undertaker, and I
said "Good evening" to him out of kindness. "Excuse us
grown folks," he said. "We got to talk." So I went up to my
room and left my fate to work itself out, since I had no
curiosity about what was destined for me, and no doubt.

10

Cain murdered Abel, and blood cried out from the earth; the house fell on Job's children, and a voice was induced or provoked into speaking from a whirlwind; and Rachel mourned for her children; and King David for Absalom. The force behind the movement of time is a mourning that will not be comforted. That is why the first event is known to have been an expulsion, and the last is hoped to be a reconciliation and return. So memory pulls us forward, so prophecy is only brilliant memory—there will be a garden where all of us as one child will sleep in our mother Eve, hooped in her ribs and staved by her spine.

Cain killed Abel, and the blood cried out from the ground—a story so sad that even God took notice of it. Maybe it was not the sadness of the story, since worse things have happened every minute since that day, but its novelty that He found striking. In the newness of the world God was a young man, and grew indignant over the slightest things. In the newness of the world God had perhaps not Himself realized the ramifications of certain of His laws, for example, that shock will spend itself in waves; that our images will mimic every gesture, and that shattered they will multiply and mimic every gesture ten, a hundred, or a thousand times. Cain, the image of God, gave the simple earth of the field a voice and a sorrow, and God Himself heard the voice, and grieved for the sorrow, so Cain was a creator, in the image of his Creator. God troubled the waters where He saw His face, and Cain became his children and their children and theirs, through a thousand generations, and all of them transients, and wherever they went everyone remembered that there had been a second creation, that the earth ran with blood and sang with sorrow. And let God purge this wicked sadness away with a flood, and let the waters recede to pools and ponds and ditches, and let every one of them mirror heaven. Still, they taste a bit of blood and hair. One cannot cup one's hand and drink from the rim of any lake without remembering that mothers have drowned in it, lifting their children toward the air, though they must have known as they did that soon enough the deluge would take all the children, too, even if their arms could have held them up. Presumably only incapacity made infants and the very old seem relatively harmless. Well, all that was purged away, and nothing is left of it after so many years but a certain pungency and savor in the water, and in the breath of creeks and lakes, which, however sad and wild, are clearly human.

I cannot taste a cup of water but I recall that the eye of the lake is my grandfather's, and that the lake's heavy, blind, encumbering waters composed my mother's limbs and weighed her garments and stopped her breath and stopped her sight. There is remembrance, and communion, altogether human and unhallowed. For families will not be broken. Curse and expel them, send their children wandering, drown them in floods and fires, and old women will make songs out of all these sorrows and sit in the porches and sing them on mild evenings. Every sorrow suggests a thousand songs, and every song recalls a thousand sorrows, and so they are infinite in number, and all the same.

Memory is the sense of loss, and loss pulls us after it. God Himself was pulled after us into the vortex we made when we fell, or so the story goes. And while He was on earth He mended families. He gave Lazarus back to his mother, and to the centurion he gave his daughter again. He even restored the severed ear of the soldier who came to arrest Him—a fact that allows us to hope the resurrection will reflect a considerable attention to detail. Yet this was no more than tinkering. Being man He felt the pull of death, and being God He must have wondered more than we do what it would be like. He is known to have walked upon water, but He was not born to drown. And when He did die it was sad—such a young man, so full of promise, and His mother wept and His friends could not believe the loss, and the story spread everywhere and the mourning would not be comforted, until He was so sharply lacked and so powerfully remembered that his friends felt Him beside them as they walked along the road, and saw someone cooking fish on the shore and knew it to be Him, and sat down to supper with Him, all wounded as He was. There is so little to remember of anyone—an anecdote, a conversation at table. But every memory is turned over and over again, every word, however chance, written in the heart in the hope that memory will fulfill itself, and become flesh, and that the wanderers will find a way home, and the perished, whose lack we always feel, will step through the door finally and stroke our hair with dreaming, habitual fondness, not having meant to keep us waiting long.

Sylvie did not want to lose me. She did not want me to

grow gigantic and multiple, so that I seemed to fill the whole house, and she did not wish me to turn subtle and miscible, so that I could pass through the membranes that separate dream and dream. She did not wish to remember me. She much preferred my simple, ordinary presence, silent and ungainly though I might be. For she could regard me without strong emotion—a familiar shape, a familiar face, a familiar silence. She could forget I was in the room. She could speak to herself, or to someone in her thoughts, with pleasure and animation, even while I sat beside her—this was the measure of our intimacy, that she gave almost no thought to me at all.

But if she lost me, I would become extraordinary by my vanishing. Imagine that my mother had come back that Sunday, say in the evening, and that she had kissed our hair and that all the necessary business of reconciliation had been transacted between her and my grandmother, and that we had sat down to supper, and Lucille and I had grown restless listening to stories about people we did not know, and had gone out to play on the chill grass in the strange, deep yard, hoping our mother would notice how late it was, and hoping she would not. Say we had driven home the whole night long, Lucille and I asleep on the back seat, cramped and aware of the chilly air that whistled through the inch of open window, diluting my mother's perfume and the smoke from her cigarettes. She might sing, "What'll I do when you are far away," or "Love letters straight from your heart," or "Cottage for sale," or "Irene." Those were her favorite songs. I remember looking at her from the back seat as we drove toward Fingerbone, the waves in the crown of her hair, the square shoulders of her good gray dress, her long hands at the top of the steering wheel, the nails gleaming a deep red. I was struck by her calm, by the elegant competence of her slightest gesture. Lucille and I had never seen her drive before, and we were very much impressed. The interior of Bernice's car smelled dusty, like an old sofa. We held on to the thick gray cord that hung across the back of the front seat and bounced up and down as if we were driving a stagecoach. The air filled with dust particles that looked like tiny bent threads, or hairs, which someone had once told us were atoms. We fought and counted horses and cemeteries, and she never spoke to us once. We asked to stop at an ice-cream stand by the road in the woods and she stopped and bought us hot fudge sundaes, and the lady there said we were nice and our mother smiled absently and said, Sometimes they are.

It seemed to me that in all this there was the hush and solemnity of incipient transfiguration. Perhaps memory is the seat not only of prophecy but of miracle as well. For it seems to me that we were recalled again and again to a sense of her calm. It seems that her quiet startled us, though she was always quiet. I remember her standing with her arms folded, pushing at the dust with the toe of her pump while she waited for us to finish our sundaes. We sat at a hot green metal table, weather-dulled and sticky, and loud black flies with rainbows in their wings fed at the pools of drying ice cream and then scrubbed their maws meticulously with their forelegs, like house cats. She was so tall and quiet in her silvery gray dress, never looking toward us, and we were sweaty and sticky and cloyed and tired of each other. I remember her, grave with the peace of the destined, the summoned, and she seems almost an apparition.

But if she had simply brought us home again to the high frame apartment building with the scaffolding of stairs, I would not remember her that way. Her eccentricities might have irked and embarrassed us when we grew older. We might have forgotten her birthday, and teased her to buy a car or to change her hair. We would have left her finally. We would have laughed together with bitterness and satisfaction at our strangely solitary childhood, in light of which our failings would seem inevitable, and all our attainments miraculous. Then we would telephone her out of guilt and nostalgia, and laugh bitterly afterward because she asked us nothing, and told us nothing, and fell silent from time to time, and was glad to get off the phone. We would take her to a restaurant and a movie on Thanksgiving and buy her best-sellers for Christmas. We would try to give her outings and make her find some interests, but she would soften and shrink in our hands, and become infirm. She would bear her infirmities with the same taut patience with which she bore our solicitude, and with which she had borne every other aspect of life, and her silence would make us more and more furious. Lucille and I would see each other often, and almost never talk of other things. Nothing would be more familiar to us than her silence, and her sad, abstracted calm. I know how it would have been, because I have observed that, in the way people are strange, they grow stranger. We would have laughed and felt abandoned and aggrieved, never knowing that she had gone all the way to the edge of the lake to rest her head and close her eyes, and had come back again for our sakes. She would have remained untransfigured. We would never have known that her calm was as slight as the skin on water, and that her calm sustained her as a coin can float on still water. We would have known nothing of the nature and reach of her sorrow if she had come back. But she left us and broke the family and the sorrow was released and we saw its wings and saw it fly a thousand ways into the hills, and sometimes I think sorrow is a predatory thing because birds scream at dawn with a marvelous terror, and there is, as I have said before, a deathly bitterness in the smell of ponds and ditches. When we were children and frightened of the dark, my grandmother used to say if we kept our eyes closed we would not see it. That was when I noticed the correspondence between the space within the circle of my skull and the space around me. I saw just the same figure against the lid of my eye or the wall of my room, or in the trees beyond my window. Even the illusion of perimeters fails when families are separated.

Sylvie realized that her first scheme to keep us together had failed. She had little hope that the hearing—which, according to a letter we received in the mail, would take place in a week's time—would turn out well. Still, she persisted in her housekeeping. She polished the windows, or those that still had panes, and the others she covered neatly with tape and brown paper. I washed the china and put it back in the cupboard and burned the boxes in the orchard. Sylvie saw the fire and came out with an armful of old magazines that had gathered in the porch. It was difficult to make them burn. Sylvie brought newspapers from the shed and we balled them up and stuck them in among the magazines and lit them with matches, and after a little while the magazines began to swell and warp and to page themselves and finally to ascend the spiraling air. That was a pretty day. The fruit trees were all bare, and their leaves on the ground were as limp and noisome as wet leather. The sky was a strong, plain blue, but the light was cool and indirect and the shadows black and precise. There seemed to be no wind at all. We could watch the heat from the fire pull and tease the air out of shape, stretching the fabric of dimension and repose with its furious ascending. The magazine pages went black, and the print and the dark parts of pictures turned silvery black. Weightless and filigreed, they spiraled to a giddy height, till some current caught them in the upper air, some high wind we could not feel assumed them. Sylvie reached up and caught a flying page on the flat of her hand. She showed it to me—in dark silver, a woman's face laughing, and below that in large letters, BETTER LATE THAN NEVER! Sylvie tried to wave the page off her hand, and the corners and edges tattered away, leaving just the laughing face, from the brows downward. She clapped her hands in the pillar of heat, and the lady ascended in cinders and motes. "There!" Sylvie said, watching them fly. She wiped her sooty hands on the flanks of her skirt. I saw the fiery transfiguration of a dog, and the bowl he ate from, and a baseball team, and a Chevrolet, and many hundreds of words. It had never occurred to me that words, too, must be salvaged, though when I thought about it, it seemed obvious. It was absurd to think that things were held in place, are held in place, by a web of words.

We burned papers and magazines until well after dark. We forgot supper. Again and again Sylvie stepped out of the firelight and in a few minutes reappeared with an armful of things to be burned. We had both become conscious of Fingerbone all around us, if not watching, then certainly aware of everything we did. Left to myself I would have shrunk under all this attention. I would have stayed in the house and read with a flashlight under the covers and have ventured out only for Wonder bread and batteries. But Sylvie reacted to her audience with a stage voice and large gestures. She kept saying, "I don't know why we didn't do this months ago," loudly, as if she thought there were listeners beyond the firelight, among the apple trees. Everything to which Sylvie imagined anyone might attach merit she did with enormous diligence and effort. We burned the entire newspaper and magazine collection that night, and soapboxes and shoeboxes, as well as almanacs and Sears catalogues and telephone books, including the current ones. Sylvie burned *Not as a Stranger*. "That isn't the sort of thing you should be reading," she said. "I don't know how it got in the house!" This was intended to impress the judicial gentlemen in the orchard, so I did not tell her it was a library book.

I loved to watch these bouts of zeal and animation—
Sylvie flushed in the firelight, prodding her whole hoard
into the quick of the fire, even the *National Geographic*
with a fold-out picture of the Taj Mahal. "We'll buy some
clothes," she said. "We'll get you something in very good
taste. Maybe a suit. You'll need it for church, anyway. And
we'll get you a permanent. When you fix yourself up, you
make a very nice impression. You really do, Ruthie." She
smiled at me across the fire. I began to imagine that Sylvie
and I might still be together after the hearing. I began to
think that the will to reform might be taken for reform itself,
not because Sylvie could ever deceive anyone, but because
her eagerness to save our household might convince them
that it should not be violated. Perhaps Sylvie and I would
trudge to church through the snow in pillbox hats. We
would sit in the last pew nearest the door, and Sylvie would
turn so she could stretch her legs. During the sermon she
would spindle the program and hum "Holy, holy, holy" and
yawn into her glove. No doubt she would attend the PTA
with commendable regularity, as well. Already she had sent
away for seeds so that she could make flower beds around
the house in the spring, and she had put a new yellow
curtain in the kitchen. Those days she cast about constantly
for ways to conform our lives to the expectations of others,
or to what she guessed their expectations might be, and she
was full of purpose, which sometimes seemed like hope. "I
ordered a turkey for Thanksgiving. I thought we could
invite Lucille. And Miss Royce, too." The fire was by now
a heap of smoldering. Sylvie tossed a stick into it, which hit
with a pneumatic *whoof!* and sent embers flying like
feathers. In the peripheries of my sight, the shadows
jumped skittishly.

"We should go in," I said. "It's cold."

"Yes," Sylvie said. "You go in and I'll put some dirt on
the ashes." By meager moonlight and firelight she walked to

the shed, and she took one of the shovels that had leaned against the wall until their tips rusted away. I stopped by the door and watched her stoke earth into the embers—one shovelful and a great waft of sparks and light rose in the air. Sylvie was all alight and around her the shadows leaped from behind their trees. A few more shovels of earth and fewer sparks flew and Sylvie stood in a duller light. Another shovelful and Sylvie and the orchard were extinguished. I sat down on the step outside the door to Sylvie's room. Sylvie did not move. I did not hear her move. I waited to see how long she would be still. I thought the darkness might make Sylvie her old self again, that she might disappear again, to extend my education, or her own. But then she stood the shovel in the ground. I could hear the rasp as the blade went into the earth, and I heard her brush her hands against the skirts of her coat—a gesture that always meant some purposeful act had been completed. She walked toward me where I sat on the step. Since the moon was on the other side of the house, I was in shadow. I thought she might not see me, so I slid to one side, off the edge of the step. Her coat almost brushed me as she passed. I heard her in the kitchen, calling "Ruthie! Ruthie!" and then I heard her steps on the stairs, and I ran into the orchard, so that I would be well hidden when it occurred to her to look out a window. And why did I run into the orchard and squat in the shadows with my hand clapped over my mouth to smother the roar of my breathing? I heard her call Ruthie, Ruthie, Ruthie, in every part of the house, turning all the lights on as she went. Then she came out on the step again and said "Ruthie!" in a loud, intimate, reproving whisper. Of course she could not go calling through the orchards and fields for me in the middle of the night. All Fingerbone would know. High hard laughter rose in my mouth and I could not stifle it all. Sylvie laughed, too. "Come in," she coaxed. "Come in where it's warm. I'll give you something good to eat." I stepped back and back through the trees and she followed me. She must have heard my steps or the rush of my breath, because wherever I went, she seemed to know. "Come in, come in where it's warm." The house stood out beyond the orchard with every one of its windows lighted. It looked large, and foreign, and contained, like a moored ship—a fantastic thing to find in a garden. I could not imagine going into it. Once there was a young girl strolling at night in an orchard. She came to a house she had never seen before, all alight so that through any window she could see curious ornaments and marvelous comforts. A door stood open, so she walked inside. It would be that kind of story, a very melancholy story. Her hair, which was as black as the sky and so long that it swept after her, a wind in the grass . . . Her fingers, which were sky black and so fine and slender that they were only cold touch, like drops of rain . . . Her step, which was so silent that people were surprised when they even thought they heard it . . . She would be transformed by the gross light into a mortal child. And when she stood at the bright window, she would find that the world was gone, the orchard was gone, her mother and grandmother and aunts were gone. Like Noah's wife on the tenth or fifteenth night of rain, she would stand in the window and realize that the world was really lost. And those outside would scarcely know her, so sadly was she changed. Before, she had been fleshed in air and clothed in nakedness and mantled in cold, and her very bones were only slender things, like shafts of ice. She had haunted the orchard out of preference, but she could walk into the lake without ripple or displacement and sail up the air as invisibly as heat. And now, lost to her kind, she would almost forget them, and she would feed coarse food to her flesh, and be almost satisfied.

I learned an important thing in the orchard that night,

which was that if you do not resist the cold, but simply relax and accept it, you no longer feel the cold as discomfort. I felt giddily free and eager, as you do in dreams, when you suddenly find that you can fly, very easily, and wonder why you have never tried it before. I might have discovered other things. For example, I was hungry enough to begin to learn that hunger has its pleasures, and I was happily at ease in the dark, and in general, I could feel that I was breaking the tethers of need, one by one. But then the sheriff came. I heard him knock. I heard him shout "Hullo?" After a minute Sylvie walked out of the orchard, quickly, toward the side door, but he came around the house and saw her on the step.

"Evening, Mrs. Fisher."

"Evening."

"Everything all right here? I seen all the lights."

"Everything's all right."

"The little girl is fine?"

"Yes, fine."

"Sleeping?"

"Yes."

"With her light on?"

"Yes, I guess so."

"I don't usually see the place all lit up like this, so late at night."

Silence. Sylvie laughed.

"Could I see the little girl?"

"What?"

"Could I see Ruthie?"

"No."

"She's upstairs sleeping?"

"Yes."

"Then it can't hurt if I peek in the door."

"She sleeps very lightly. She'll wake up."

"I'll go up in my stockings, ma'am. It won't be no bother, I promise."

Silence.

"Where is she, Mrs. Fisher?"

"Around the house somewhere."

"Well, I'll step in and say good evening to her."

"She's not inside, she's outside."

The sheriff fingered the brim of his hat. "Where?"

"Probably in the orchard. I was looking for her."

"You can't find her?"

"She won't let me. It's like a game."

I walked out of the orchard and went and stood on the porch beside Sylvie.

"Ruthie," the sheriff asked, "would you like to come to my house tonight? You know, I got grandchildren myself. We got lots of room. The missus would be happy for the company. I'm just on my way to Lewiston. They got the Cranshaw boy we been looking for. Stold a car down there . . ."

"I want to stay here."

"You're sure, now."

"Yes."

The sheriff shifted his considerable weight. "What were you doing out in the cold with no coat on, in the middle of the night, with school tomorrow?"

I said nothing.

"Come on home with me."

"No!"

"We're nice folks, you know. My wife's some cook, I tell you. We got apple pie at our house, Ruthie, the world's finest, believe me!"

"No!"

" 'No, thank you,' " Sylvie said.

"No, thank you."

"Well. All right, then. But I don't have to tell you to get to bed now, do I?"

"No."

"All right. But I'm going to be keeping an eye on you. I want you in school tomorrow, you hear?"

"Yes."

"Good night."

"Good night."

"See you tomorrow," the sheriff said, and walked to his car. "I want you to be here tomorrow, now. I want to talk to you tomorrow," he called back to us.

11

The house was as dank as the orchard, and would *not* burn. Oh, the doilies on the couch blazed a while, and they left smoldering rings on the arms, but Sylvie slapped those out with her hand, saying they were worse than nothing. We had turned out all the lights as soon as the sheriff was gone, and so it seemed as if something fantastic were happening in the house. One moment I had no idea where Sylvie was, and the next moment the parlor curtains were a sheet of flames and Sylvie was kneeling in front of them, dull rose in the light with a black shadow behind her. But the curtains were consumed in moments and fell to the floor and went out. "Damn!" Sylvie said, and we laughed, but as little as we could, because we knew it was a solemn thing to burn a house down. To any other eye we might have seemed wild and pranking, unhuman spirits in the house, to whom lampshades and piano scarves were noth-

ing, but that was only because we were in such haste and
breathing was difficult.

Sylvie and I (I think that night we were almost a single
person) could not leave that house, which was stashed like
a brain, a reliquary, its relics to be pawed and sorted and
parceled out among the needy and the parsimonious of
Fingerbone. Imagine the blank light of Judgment falling on
you suddenly. It would be like that. For even things lost in
a house abide, like forgotten sorrows and incipient dreams,
and many household things are of purely sentimental value,
like the dim coil of thick hair, saved from my grandmother's
girlhood, which was kept in a hatbox on top of the
wardrobe, along with my mother's gray purse. In the equal
light of disinterested scrutiny such things are not themselves. They are transformed into pure object, and are
horrible, and must be burned.

For we had to leave. I could not stay, and Sylvie would
not stay without me. Now truly we were cast out to wander,
and there was an end to housekeeping. Sylvie set fire to the
straw of the broom, and held it blazing to the hem of the
pantry curtain, and to the fringe of the rug, so there were
two good fires, but then we heard a train whistle, and Sylvie
said, "We have to run! Get your coat!" I did, and pulled on
my boots. Sylvie put three bags of bread under her arm, and
threw the broom at the woodpile, and took my hand, and
we ran out the door into the orchard, which was very dark
and cold, and across the garden, which was hilled and
furrowed and full of the muck and stubble of slain vegetables. Just as we reached the edge of the fallow field that lay
between the garden and the tracks, the train passed in front
of us and disappeared. "Oh, no!" Sylvie said. The air was
sharp and cold and painful to swallow. Then bang! we
could hear a window shatter in the house behind us, and
bang! another. Someone shouted. We turned around to see,
but we saw neither flames nor smoke. "It wasn't a good

enough fire," Sylvie said. "They'll find out right away we're not inside, and they'll come looking for us. What a mess."

"We'll hide in the woods."

"They'll use dogs."

We were still for a while, listening to the shouts and watching the lights come on in the neighboring houses. We could even hear children's voices, and there was an uproar among the dogs.

"One thing we could do," Sylvie said. Her voice was low and exulting.

"What?"

"Cross the bridge."

"Walk."

"Dogs wouldn't dare follow, and nobody'd believe them anyway. Nobody's ever done that. Crossed the bridge. Not that anybody knows of."

Well.

"We've got to go if we're going," Sylvie said. "Are you all buttoned up? You should have a hat." She put her arm around my shoulder and squeezed me. She whispered, "It's not the worst thing, Ruthie, drifting. You'll see. You'll see."

It was a dark and clouded night, but the tracks led to the lake like a broad path. Sylvie walked in front of me. We stepped on every other tie, although that made our stride uncomfortably long, because stepping on every tie made it uncomfortably short. But it was easy enough. I followed after Sylvie with slow, long, dancer's steps, and above us the stars, dim as dust in their Babylonian multitudes, pulled through the dark along the whorls of an enormous vortex— for that is what it is, I have seen it in pictures—were invisible, and the moon was long down. I could barely see Sylvie. I could barely see where I put my feet. Perhaps it was only the certainty that she was in front of me, and that I need only put my foot directly before me, that made me think I saw anything at all.

"What if a train comes?" I asked.

And she answered, "There's no train till morning."

I could feel the bridge rising, and then suddenly a watery wind blew up my legs and billowed my coat, and more than that, there were the sliding and shimmering sounds of the water, quiet sounds but wide—if you dive under water and stay down till your breath gives out, when you come up into the air again, you hear space and distance. It was like that. A wave turned a stick or a stone on some black beach how many miles away, and I heard it at my ear. To be suddenly above the water was a giddy thing, an elation, and made me uncertain of my steps. I had to think of other things. I thought of the house behind me, all turned to fire, and the fire leaping and whirling in its own fierce winds. Imagine the spirit of the house breaking out the windows and knocking down the doors, and all the neighbors astonished at the sovereign ease with which it burst its tomb, broke up its grave. Bang! and the clay that had held the shape of the Chinese jar was shattered, and the jar was a whirl in the air, ascending . . . bang! and the bureau mirror fell in shivers the shape of flame and had nothing to show but fire. Every last thing would turn to flame and ascend, so cleanly would the soul of the house escape, and all Fingerbone would come marveling to see the smoldering place where its foot had last rested.

I did not dare to turn my head to see if the house was burning. I was afraid that if I turned at all I would lose my bearings and misstep. It was so dark there might have been no Sylvie ahead of me, and the bridge might have created itself under my foot as I walked, and vanished again behind me.

But I could hear the bridge. It was wooden, and it creaked. It leaned in the slow rhythm that moves things in water. The current pulled it south, and under my feet I could feel it drift south ever so slightly, and then right itself again. This rhythm seemed to be its own. It had nothing to do, as far as I could tell, with the steady rush of water toward the river. The slow creaking made me think of a park by the water where my mother used to take Lucille and me. It had a swing built of wood, as high as a scaffold and loose in all its joints, and when my mother pushed me the scaffold leaned after me, and creaked. That was where she sat me on her shoulders so that I could paddle my hands in the chestnut leaves, so cool, and that was the day we bought hamburgers at a white cart for supper and sat on a green bench by the seawall feeding all the bread to the sea gulls and watching the ponderous ferries sail between sky and water so precisely the same electric blue that there was no horizon. The horns of the ferries made huge, delicate sounds, like cows lowing. They should have left a milky breath in the air. I thought they did, but that was just the sound lingering. My mother was happy that day, we did not know why. And if she was sad the next, we did not know why. And if she was gone the next, we did not know why. It was as if she righted herself continually against some current that never ceased to pull. She swayed continuously, like a thing in water, and it was graceful, a slow dance, a sad and heady dance.

Sylvie has, pinned to the underside of her right lapel, a newspaper clipping with the heading, LAKE CLAIMS TWO. It is so long that she had to fold it several times before she put the pin in. It describes our attempt to burn the house. It explains that there was soon to have been a custody hearing—neighbors were alarmed by increasingly erratic behavior. "We should have seen this coming," one area man remarked. (Mention is made of the fact that my mother had died in the lake, also an apparent suicide.) Dogs traced us to the bridge. Townspeople began searching at dawn for the bodies, but we were never found, never found, and the search was at last abandoned.

It happened many years ago, now, and the worst of it is that in all those years we have never contacted Lucille. At first we were afraid we would be found if we tried to telephone her or send a note. "After seven years they can't get you for anything," Sylvie said, and seven years passed, but we both knew they could always get you for increasingly erratic behavior, and Sylvie, and I, too, have that to fear. We are drifters. And once you have set your foot in that path it is hard to imagine another one. Now and then I take a job as a waitress, or a clerk, and it is pleasant for a while. Sylvie and I see all the movies. But finally the imposture becomes burdensome, and obvious. Customers begin to react to my smile as if it were a grimace, and suddenly something in my manner makes them count their change. If I had the choice, I would work in a truck stop. I like to overhear the stories strangers tell each other, and I like the fastidious pleasure solitary people take in the smallest details of their small comforts. In rain or hard weather they set their elbows on the counter and ask what kind of pie you have, just to hear the long old litany again. But after a while, when the customers and the waitresses and the dishwasher and the cook have told me, or said in my hearing, so much about themselves that my own silence seems suddenly remarkable, then they begin to suspect me, and it is as if I put a chill on the coffee by serving it. What have I to do with these ceremonies of sustenance, of nurturing? They begin to ask why I do not eat anything myself. It would put meat on your bones, they say. Once they begin to look at me like that, it is best that I leave.

When did I become so unlike other people? Either it was when I followed Sylvie across the bridge, and the lake claimed us, or it was when my mother left me waiting for her, and established in me the habit of waiting and expectation which makes any present moment most significant for what it does not contain. Or it was at my conception.

Of my conception I know only what you know of yours.
It occurred in darkness and I was unconsenting. I (and that
slenderest word is too gross for the rare thing I was then)
walked forever through reachless oblivion, in the mood of
one smelling night-blooming flowers, and suddenly— My
ravishers left their traces in me, male and female, and over
the months I rounded, grew heavy, until the scandal could
no longer be concealed and oblivion expelled me. But this
I have in common with all my kind. By some bleak
alchemy what had been mere unbeing becomes death when
life is mingled with it. So they seal the door against our
returning.

Then there is the matter of my mother's abandonment of
me. Again, this is the common experience. They walk
ahead of us, and walk too fast, and forget us, they are so lost
in thoughts of their own, and soon or late they disappear.
The only mystery is that we expect it to be otherwise.

I believe it was the crossing of the bridge that changed me
finally. The terrors of the crossing were considerable. Twice
I stumbled and fell. And a wind came up from the north, so
that the push of the wind and the pull of the current were
the same, and it seemed as though they were not to be
resisted. And then it was so dark.

Something happened, something so memorable that
when I think back to the crossing of the bridge, one
moment bulges like the belly of a lens and all the others are
at the peripheries and diminished. Was it only that the wind
rose suddenly, so that we had to cower and lean against it
like blind women groping their way along a wall? or did we
really hear some sound too loud to be heard, some word so
true we did not understand it, but merely felt it pour
through our nerves like darkness or water?

I have never distinguished readily between thinking and
dreaming. I know my life would be much different if I could
ever say, This I have learned from my senses, while that I

have merely imagined. I will try to tell you the plain truth. Sylvie and I walked the whole black night across the railroad bridge at Fingerbone—a very long bridge, as you know if you have seen it—and we were obliged to walk slowly, by the wind and by darkness. In simple truth, we were not far from shore when dawn came, and we clambered down onto the rocks just before the eastbound rumbled out of the woods and across the bridge toward Fingerbone. We caught the next westbound and drowsed among poultry crates all the way to Seattle. From there we went to Portland, and from there to Crescent City, and from there to Vancouver, and from there to Seattle. At first our trail was intricate so that we would elude discovery, and then it was intricate because we had no particular reason to go to one town rather than another, and no particular reason to stay anywhere, or to leave.

Sylvie and I are not travelers. We talk sometimes about San Francisco, but we have never gone there. Sylvie still has friends in Montana, so now and then we pass through Fingerbone on the way to Butte or Billings or Deer Lodge. We stand in the door to watch for the lake, and then to watch it pass, and to try to catch a glimpse of the old house, but we cannot see it from the tracks. Someone is living there. Someone has pruned the apple trees and taken out the dead ones and restrung the clothesline and patched the shed roof. Someone plants sunflowers and giant dahlias at the foot of the garden. I imagine it is Lucille, fiercely neat, stalemating the forces of ruin. I imagine doilies, high and stiff, and a bright pantry curtain, there to rebuke us with newness and a smell of starch whenever we might wander in the door. But I know Lucille is not there. She has gone to some city, and won the admiration of skeptics by the thoroughness, the determination, with which she does whatever it is she does. Once, Sylvie called information in Boston and asked if Lucille Stone had a number listed there. Lawrence, Linda, and Lucas, the operator said, but no Lucille. So we do not know where she is, or how to find her. "She's probably married," Sylvie says, and no doubt she is. Someday when I am feeling presentable I will go into Fingerbone and make inquiries. I must do it soon, for such days are rare now.

All this is fact. Fact explains nothing. On the contrary, it is fact that requires explanation. For example, I pass again and again behind my grandmother's house, and never get off at the station and walk back to see if it is still the same house, altered perhaps by the repairs the fire made necessary, or if it is a new house built on the old site. I would like to see the people who live there. Seeing them would expel poor Lucille, who has, in my mind, waited there in a fury of righteousness, cleansing and polishing, all these years. She thinks she hears someone on the walk, and hurries to open the door, too eager to wait for the bell. It is the mailman, it is the wind, it is nothing at all. Sometimes she dreams that we come walking up the road in our billowing raincoats, hunched against the cold, talking together in words she cannot quite understand. And when we look up and speak to her the words are smothered, and their intervals swelled, and their cadences distended, like sounds in water. What if I should walk to the house one night and find Lucille there? It is possible. Since we are dead, the house would be hers now. Perhaps she is in the kitchen, snuggling pretty daughters in her lap, and perhaps now and then they look at the black window to find out what their mother seems to see there, and they see their own faces and a face so like their mother's, so rapt and full of tender watching, that only Lucille could think the face was mine. If Lucille is there, Sylvie and I have stood outside her window a thousand times, and we have thrown the side door open when she was upstairs changing beds, and we have brought in leaves, and flung the curtains and tipped the bud vase, and somehow left the house again before she could run downstairs, leaving behind us a strong smell of lake water. She would sigh and think, "They never change."

Or imagine Lucille in Boston, at a table in a restaurant, waiting for a friend. She is tastefully dressed—wearing, say, a tweed suit with an amber scarf at the throat to draw attention to the red in her darkening hair. Her water glass has left two-thirds of a ring on the table, and she works at completing the circle with her thumbnail. Sylvie and I do not flounce in through the door, smoothing the skirts of our oversized coats and combing our hair back with our fingers. We do not sit down at the table next to hers and empty our pockets in a small damp heap in the middle of the table, and sort out the gum wrappers and ticket stubs, and add up the coins and dollar bills, and laugh and add them up again. My mother, likewise, is not there, and my grand-mother in her house slippers with her pigtail wagging, and my grandfather, with his hair combed flat against his brow, does not examine the menu with studious interest. We are nowhere in Boston. However Lucille may look, she will never find us there, or any trace or sign. We pause nowhere in Boston, even to admire a store window, and the perim-eters of our wandering are nowhere. No one watching this woman smear her initials in the steam on her water glass with her first finger, or slip cellophane packets of oyster crackers into her handbag for the sea gulls, could know how her thoughts are thronged by our absence, or know how she does not watch, does not listen, does not wait, does not hope, and always for me and Sylvie.

ABOUT THE AUTHOR

MARILYNNE ROBINSON lives in Northampton, Massachusetts, with her husband and two sons. *Housekeeping* is her first novel, and her second book, *Mother Country*, will be published in 1989.